THE AUGUST HOUSE BOOK OF
SCARY STORIES

Spooky Tales for Telling Out Loud

edited by Liz Parkhurst

August House, Inc.
ATLANTA

Published 2009 by August House, Inc.,
3500 Piedmont Road NE, Suite 310
Atlanta, GA 30305
404-442-4420
http://www.augusthouse.com

Book design by H. K. Stewart
Illustrations by Tom Wrenn

Manufactured in the United States
10 9 8 7 6 5 4 3 2 1

LIBRARY OF CONGRESS CATALOGING-IN-PUBLICATION DATA
The August House book of scary stories : spooky tales for telling out loud / edited by Liz Parkhurst.
    v. cm.
  Summary: An anthology of spooky stories drawn from folklore, local history, and the storytellers' imaginations, and divided into the categories "Just Desserts and Lessons Learned," "Ghostly Guardians," "Dark Humor," "Urban Legends and Jump Tales," and "Fearless Females."
  ISBN 978-0-87483-915-9 (hardcover : alk. paper) 1. Children's stories. 2. Horror tales. [1. Short stories. 2. Horror stories. 3. Storytelling—Collections.] I. Parkhurst, Liz Smith.
  PZ5.A86 2009
  [Fic]—dc22
                                                    2009008711

Contents

Dark Humor

Urban Legends and Jump Tales

Fearless Females

Just Deserts
and Lessons Learned

Mean John and the Jack-o-lantern

An Irish Folktale
Michael J. Caduto

Ablacksmith named John once lived at the edge of the Irish moors. Though he was as strong as an oak, people often said, "That John has a chip on his shoulder and a sour taste in his mouth."

Children loved to play pranks on old John. They waited until he sat down to eat lunch. Then the bravest child would run into his shop, bang the hammer and anvil, and run back down the path.

"Leave my hammer alone!" John would bellow through the door.

Children knew that Mean John hated the creak of his rocking chair. As John worked, a child would quietly slip inside, rock that chair until it creaked, then bolt to the safety of the woods.

"Stay out of my rocking chair!" Mean John would yell, shaking his fist.

Sometimes, passersby could not coax their horses up the steep hill nearby. Often, they would break off a piece of the thornbush that grew by John's front door and use it as a switch.

John would run from his shop and chase them down the road. "You leave my thornbush alone!" he would scream after them.

☠☠☠

Back in those days, every All Hallows' Eve, folks in Ireland, Scotland, and England believed that the souls of the dead who were trapped in Purgatory wandered about the places where they had once lived. On that very night, Saint Peter visited Earth disguised as an old beggar. He wore old rags, had a long scraggly beard, and leaned on a crooked cane.

One Halloween, Saint Peter knocked on Mean John's door. When John answered, Saint Peter said, "I am an old hungry beggar. Please give me something to eat."

"Be gone!" said John. "I've got work to do and my own mouth to feed."

"But I am tired and hungry and cold," Saint Peter persisted.

"Very well," said Mean John slyly. He swung the old man into his chair and gave him a plate of dried-up beans and a moldy crust of bread.

Suddenly, the beggar's clothes turned a glistening white and his gnarly cane changed into a golden staff. He grew so tall that his shining white hair touched the ceiling. Mean John did not recognize the visage that stood before him, for he had never been known to enjoy the company of saints.

"Don't you know me, John?"

"No, I have never seen your kind," said Mean John in a voice that quivered with fear.

"I am Saint Peter. One night each year I come to Earth dressed as a beggar. The first person who gives me a meal is granted three wishes."

"And what of me?" asked John.

"You are a lost soul, but I must honor my pledge. What do you desire?"

"Whenever someone picks up that hammer," answered John, "I want it to stick in their hands and keep swinging until I say it can stop."

"You have a heart of stone," said Saint Peter.

"And whenever someone rocks in that chair, I want it to hold them down and keep rocking, faster and faster, until I tell it to let them go."

"John, you tortured spirit."

"And every time a person steals a piece of my thornbush, I want the branches to pull them into the thorns until I tell it to release them."

"You are the meanest person I have ever met," Saint Peter exclaimed, "but so be it. Here are your three twisted wishes," he said, waving his staff in disgust.

Mean John saw a blinding flash. When the light had vanished, Saint Peter was gone.

The next day, when one of the boys snuck into Mean John's shop and grabbed his hammer, it stuck in the boy's hand and swung with a life of its own.

"Please make it stop!" the boy begged.

"Are you going to go away and never come back?" asked Mean John.

"Yes, yes, whatever you say!" cried the terrified little boy.

"Let him go," Mean John told the hammer.

As soon as the hammer released his arm, the boy fled through the door, crying.

The next afternoon, while Mean John was working, a little girl stole into the shop, sat in his chair, and rocked until it creaked. As she did so, the chair held her fast and began to rock faster and faster.

"Make it stop!" she screamed.

"Only if you leave me alone for good," said John.

"I wi-i-i-i-i-ill," she said, her voice wavering as the chair rocked furiously.

"Let her go," shouted John to the chair. The chair threw the girl off the seat and out the door.

That same evening, a horse stopped cold in front of Mean John's house. When the driver broke a switch from the thornbush, he was instantly drawn into the wicked branches. The more he struggled, the deeper the thorns pricked his skin. "Help!" he cried. "Someone help me!"

Mean John came to the door. "Will you leave my thornbush alone and never set foot in this yard again?"

"Yes," said the driver. "Please, make it let go."

"Release him," said John, and the thornbush parted. The man ran to his horse and galloped away in a cloud of dust.

☠☠☠

Mean John's reputation spread all the way down through the deep fissures of the earth until it reached the eternal heat and fires of the underworld. There, hidden behind a towering iron gate that glowed red from the lapping flames within, was the Devil's realm.

One day someone in the Devil's domain said, "That John is the meanest thing that ever lived."

The Devil was furious. "What did you say?" he cried in a voice that shook the bowels of his blazing kingdom and rattled the ground above. "No one can be meaner than the Devil. I will not have it!"

The Devil set out to find Mean John. Higher and higher he climbed, passing through hot, steaming crevasses from whose roofs hung fang-like teeth of stone. He drove upward until he reached the cool, damp caves where bats fled in fear before him. By the time the Devil stood at Mean John's door it was midnight. His knock rang like thunder.

"What?" John exclaimed when he opened the door. "Has All Hallows' Eve come so soon? What a convincing costume." There, before him, stood an enormous creature the color of fire. He had great curling horns and a forked tail that flicked like the tongue of a snake.

"You are coming with me, John," said the Devil in a deep voice. "They say that you are meaner than me, and that cannot stand. The only place I can keep watch over you is down in the underworld."

"No one tells me what to do!" said John.

"We'll see about that," replied the Devil as he plunged through the door and took Mean John by the collar.

"You're so weak you couldn't lift that hammer," laughed John.

"Like this?" said the Devil as he grabbed the handle. To his surprise, his arm was jerked up and down as the hammer struck the anvil, faster and faster.

"Stop this thing!" cried the Devil.

"Are you going to leave me alone?"

"Yes, yes!" answered the Devil.

"Let him go," Mean John told the hammer.

But as soon as the hammer released the Devil's arm, the Devil lunged at Mean John and wrestled him.

"You said you would leave," cried Mean John.

"I'm the Devil. Only a fool would believe what I say!"

Mean John rolled on his back and threw the Devil into his chair, which held the Devil and began to rock, faster and faster.

"Plea-ea-ea-ea-ease," said the Devil as his head whipped back and forth. "Make it stop!"

"*Promise* me that you will go away and leave me be," said Mean John.

"I wi-i-i-i-ill," said the Devil. "Help me!"

"Stop!" said John. Abruptly, the chair stopped rocking.

The Devil again came toward Mean John. "You promised to leave!" yelled John.

"And I will," said the Devil, "on one last condition."

"What?"

"That you beat me in wrestling."

John threw himself across the room and into the Devil's knees.

"Aargh!" cried the Devil as he lifted John's feet and swung him around.

With a mighty effort Mean John gained his footing and threw the Devil through the front door. Then Mean John rolled the Devil into the thornbush.

The Devil writhed in pain as the thorns cut him. "Please! I beg you, get me out of here!" he screamed.

"Convince me that you will leave!" screamed John.

"If I don't leave, may I be thrown into an icy sea and my flames go out forever."

"Let him go!" yelled Mean John to the thornbush.

With a cry of anguish the Devil flew away from Mean John's house and didn't stop until he passed through the glowing gates of the underworld.

Word spread far and wide that Mean John had defeated the Devil. No one ever knocked on Mean John's door again. Time passed, and even Mean John discovered that he was mortal. One day he raised his hammer for the last time and fell over with his final breath.

Mean John's spirit wandered from his house. *Where will I go?* he thought. *I have been unkind, I know, but perhaps Saint Peter will forgive me.*

Soon, Mean John was in Heaven, knocking on the pearly gates. The great stone gates swung open with a deep grinding sound. There stood Saint Peter himself.

"Mean John, how dare you bring your stone-cold heart to the gates of Heaven? You had your chance many years ago!"

"But I just thought—"

"Be gone!" cried Saint Peter as he swung the gates closed with a rumble.

Maybe I am meant to be with my own kind, thought Mean John. Down, down, down he went until he found himself staring up at the towering iron gate that led to the underworld. The crackle and roar of fire and the smell of smoke filled the air. Strange shadows danced on the stone walls.

Mean John knocked. The doors swung open with the sound of screeching metal. Tongues of flame shot out toward Mean John as he tried to shield his face with his hands. The Devil loomed over him with eyes of glowing coals and iron claws that clutched the handle of the door to the underworld, which was shaped like the head of a serpent. The Devil seemed made of living flames that curled and writhed into the twisted form of a hideous creature.

"What?" exclaimed the Devil with a tongue of fire. "John? Are you mad? You ruined my reputation as the meanest being who ever lived, and now you show up at my door to mock me!"

John tried to speak, but the blast of heat that entered his lungs choked him. The Devil swung the doors closed with a ring that buckled John's knees.

John climbed up to the surface of Earth. He wandered afar— a lost soul with no friends in the world. Sometimes, even today, if you go to the lonely moors and marshlands you might see a faint light that hovers just above the water, or an unseen figure that swirls the mist as it drifts by. It is Mean John's spirit—forever lost and searching for a place to rest.

Every All Hallows' Eve, Mean John, whose nickname is "Jack," wanders among the lost ghosts, ghouls, and goblins in search of a home. After the sun goes down on Halloween, flickering jack-o'-lanterns frighten Mean John away. Make the face of your jack-o'-lantern as scary as you can, or Mean John might come knocking on your door.

Story Notes

"Mean John" is the first story that I ever told to children and is still the most popular tale in my program of scary stories. There is nothing

subtle about it, which is part of its allure for both children and adults. Whenever I tell this story I put everything I have into each personality, voice, and scene. The three main characters—Mean John, Saint Peter, and the Devil—appear in places as far afield as Heaven and Hades, and as dark as a blacksmith's forge and a lonely nocturnal marsh. The realms of "Mean John" offer no end of opportunities for evoking drama and creative effect when sharing this story.

My version is based on an old Irish folktale of an unkind blacksmith. This ending reveals why we carve and illuminate frightening faces on jack-o'-lanterns. Other versions end with "Mean Jack" haunting the dark places with nothing to light the way but a bit of marsh gas set inside a hollowed-out turnip, gourd, potato, or pumpkin.

After you tell the story, ask audience members to share what they think the story means and inquire whether it reminds them of other traditional folklore they've heard in the past. As the ultimate cautionary tale, "Mean John" evokes the timeless adage, "What goes around, comes around."

MICHAEL J. CADUTO is an author, storyteller, ecologist, and musician who once used CPR to save a chipmunk's life. He has traveled throughout the world presenting environmental and cultural performances and workshops for all age. His numerous books and recordings, including Earth Tales from Around the World and the Keepers of the Earth series (co-creator and author), have been honored with the American Folklore Society's Aesop Prize, the NAPPA Gold and Silver awards, the Storytelling World Award, Skipping Stones Honor Award, and the ASCAP Popular Award. He lives in Norwich, Vermont. His website is www.p-e-a-c-e.net.

The Vain Girl and the Handsome Visitor

Based on a Mexican Urban Legend
Olga Loya

My grandmother Goya used to pass on dichos—*sayings—and tell stories to teach lessons. Since I was a very mischievous little girl, I did not want to listen to her stories. When she would start to tell a story or repeat a saying, I would try to get out of there. If I could not leave, I simply would not pay attention. I was never obvious about it, or I would have gotten in trouble for being disrespectful. I just drifted in my mind.*

When I started traveling around telling stories, different versions of this story kept getting told. Everyone tells this story as though it happened in their village, so it is treated as a sort of urban legend in many Latino communities. One woman told a version where the building fell down. She said to the group, "And if you don't believe me, you can go to my village and see the rubble of that building!"

As I heard this story over and over, I realized I had heard it long before. It was one of the stories my grandmother had told many times.

Once in a small village in Mexico, there lived a very beautiful young woman named Evita. She had long dark hair, big brown eyes with long eyelashes, and beautiful red lips. There was a problem, though. She knew she was beautiful.

She would look in the mirror and say, "Ay, *soy tan hermosa.* Oh, I am so beautiful."

Then she would open her eyes wide and flutter her eyelashes and say, "*Y mis ojos son tan hermosos*. And my eyes are so beautiful."

Then she would smile into the mirror and say, "*Mi sonrisa es tan bonita con mis dientes blancos*. My smile is so pretty with my white teeth."

Her mother would watch with concern. "You shouldn't do that, Evita," she would say. "You should have more humility. *Vas a ver*. You will see."

Oh, *máma*, why can't I say that? You know and I know that I am beautiful!"

Whenever Evita walked along the road and noticed a young man watching her, she would flutter her eyelashes at him and he would almost faint. If she wanted to drive one of the young men crazy, she would swing her long beautiful black braid from one side to the other while she looked at him. Sometimes, if the young man was sitting on a fence, he fell off.

All the men sighed because they were very interested in her.

Every Sunday everyone in the village—young and old— would go to the *tardeada*, afternoon dance.

One by one, the young men came over to ask her to dance. She would look them up and down and then say, "*No gracias, no, ni modo*. No thank you, no way." She'd mumble to herself, "*Demasiado alto, demasiado corto, demasiado flaco, demasiado gordo*. Too tall, too short, too skinny, too fat."

Her mother would say to her, "You should not act like that. *Vas a ver*. You will see."

Evita did not say anything. But she thought to herself, *Why should I be humble? I am beautiful*.

One Sunday afternoon a very handsome stranger walked in while the *tardeada* was underway. He was tall with a beautiful smile. His clothes were all black. He wore a hat and boots with silver trim.

Evita took one look at him and said to all the girls, "He's mine!"

But the stranger did not dance with her. He asked other young women to dance but did not so much as look her way. Everyone noticed what was going on and whispered to each other.

Evita went home quite stunned. *How could this happen?* she thought to herself. *I am the most beautiful in all the village. I will make him ask me to dance. I will make myself a dress so beautiful that he will not be able to resist me!*

She worked all week on a beautiful yellow silk dress with a full skirt and off-the-shoulder sleeves. She did not sleep very much that next week because that handsome stranger walked through her dreams in his black and silver boots.

That next Sunday, she wore her yellow silk dress. She wore her braid up in a crown with a yellow flower in it. She carried a fan of many colors in front of her as she walked into the *tardeada*. When she walked in, all the men, young and old, stared at her with their mouths hanging open.

Everyone waited anxiously to see what was going to happen.

The handsome man finally arrived. He walked in and stood at the door looking at everyone. Everyone looked at the handsome stranger, and then they looked at Evita. Then he began to dance with everyone around her again. Evita sat with her head lowered, gazing at the ground and trying not to look at him. She could not believe that he was not asking her to dance or even coming close to her.

By this time everyone was watching and whispering and giggling behind their hands.

"Did you see? He didn't ask Evita to dance," the other girls giggled. "He didn't ask Evita to dance!"

Again Evita went home wondering about this handsome, mysterious man. She thought, *I will make myself a beautiful red dress that he will not be able to resist!*

That next week Evita worked night and day on her new dress. She did not dream of the stranger very much because she could not sleep. But every waking moment she kept wondering about him.

That next Sunday, Evita dressed in her beautiful red dress. She took her hair down, and it flowed down her back in cascades. When she walked into the *tardeada*, everyone stopped to look at her. The men all sighed at the same time.

Again, the mysterious handsome man appeared. He did just as he had done before. Ignoring Evita, he danced with all the other young women, including her own sisters. *Why is he dancing with everyone else?* she asked herself. *I am the most beautiful girl in the village!*

But tonight was different. On the very last dance, he came over to her. He extended his hand and said, "*Un baile por favor,* a dance please." Evita stood up, took his hand, and they began to dance. It was just as she had dreamed. They fit perfectly together. He spun her around and around, and she felt as though she were floating. Her eyes were closed, and she was enjoying the dance a great deal.

Suddenly she heard a scream. She looked around and saw people running and screaming through the dance hall. She looked up at the handsome man … but he wasn't so handsome anymore. Now horns were coming out of his head and his eyes were red. She was terrified. As she screamed she leaned farther back and saw that he had a tail and that his feet had claws like a rooster's.

Evita realized that she and this terrible stranger were floating off the ground. She pushed away from him with all her might and made him lose his balance. When she fell to the ground, she scrambled to her feet and ran as fast as she could, but she could hear him chasing her from behind and screaming, "Evita! Evita!" He was catching up with her, and she could almost feel his breath on her back as he screamed, "Evita! Evita! Evita!"

She ran to the only place she could think of to go. She reached the church, dashed through the door, and locked it behind her.

He banged on the door and screamed, "Evita, come out of there! Evita! Evita!"

He banged and called out her name many times.

Evita sat in the church, praying and crying. She was so scared. Finally he left.

In a while she heard a knock on the door. "Open the door, Evita."

It sounded like her mother, but she said, "How do I know it is you?"

The voice said, "Evita, *yo te dije*—I told you."

Evita knew it was her mother. She opened the door and fell into her mother's arms, sobbing with relief.

After that day, Evita danced with everyone who asked her to dance. She was much more gentle and kind to everyone too.

The strange visitor never returned, but Evita never ever forgot him.

Story Notes

This is a fun story to tell because Evita is so conceited. I flutter my eyelashes and swing my head back and forth when she is walking down the street. It is fun to play up the gossiping among the girls, with a little more laughter and talking every time the visitor ignores Evita. I also love the sequence of the men's reaction to her; sometimes I prompt the audience to react with me, mouths open followed by deep sighs. In performance, my favorite part is when the visitor is chasing her and calling out to her in a deep strong voice—"Evita!"—over and over again. Be sure to pause every time he calls her name; it makes it scarier and creates suspense.

Nationally known Latina storyteller, performance artist, keynote speaker, and author OLGA LOYA dramatically mixes Spanish and

English in her performances. Her repertoire demonstrates how diversity embraces the richness of cultures in the commonality and individuality of our lives. She has been a featured teller at many festivals, including the Guadalajara Festival and the National Storytelling Festival. She is the author of *Momentos Mágicos/Magic Moments*, winner of the Aesop Accolade Award and included on the Américas Commended List. She lives in San Jose, California.

The Gingerbread Boy

A Kentucky Folktale
Mary Hamilton

There once lived a girl who shared a home with her stepmother. Years earlier, her mother had died, and her father had remarried. While her father lived, her stepmother treated her kindly. But after the girl's father died, that woman turned poison mean. She made the girl do all the work around the house and on the farm. When the girl didn't work fast enough—and most days there was no fast enough—the woman beat the girl with a chain. The girl was miserable, but she had nowhere else to go.

One morning, when the girl was around fourteen years old, her stepmother said, "Today you are going to chop the weeds out of the cotton. Go on out there, and don't come back to the house until you've finished, either." She sent the girl out without any breakfast.

The girl trudged out to the shed, picked up a hoe, and walked on down to the cotton patch, where she began chopping weeds. The girl chopped and chopped. The sun beat down on her. Her stomach growled. Still, she chopped. But as she worked, she thought: *I ought to just run away, but where would I go?*

The longer she worked, the more running away seemed like a reasonable idea. Finally, she gave in. She hid the hoe in tall weeds under an old wagon. Then she walked into some nearby woods.

Now, even though the woods were so close that the girl could hear leaves rustle in the slightest breeze, she had never been there before. Her stepmother kept her working so hard; she'd never even had time to explore the woods right next to the fields. So in no time she was lost, but that didn't stop her. *I'd rather die out here than go back,* she thought, and she kept walking.

About mid-afternoon, she reached a clearing. In front of her stood an amazing house. The shutters were made of wafer cookies, and gumdrops studded the walls. Oh, the girl was so hungry, she couldn't stop herself. She ran up to a window, broke off a bit of shutter, and popped it into her mouth.

The door of the house opened, and an old woman looked out. "Child," she said, "you must be awfully hungry if you're chewing up my house."

The girl swallowed hastily. "I'm sorry, ma'am," she apologized. "I should never have done that. I am so sorry."

"It's alright, child," said the old woman. "You've done no harm that can't be undone. Like I said, you must be awfully hungry." The old woman offered her hand. "Come on inside, and let me feed you a proper meal."

The girl went inside, and the old woman did indeed feed her a fine meal. The old woman also told the girl stories and jokes. The two of them talked and laughed together. The girl felt a joy she had not known since her mother died.

Then the old woman glanced out the window. "Oh child, it's going to be dark soon," she said. "You need to go on home now."

"Oh," sighed the girl, "do I have to go? Couldn't I stay with you?"

"No, you need to go home."

"But—"

The old woman interrupted her. "I know you're living a hard life, but you have to go home."

"I was lost when I found your house," the girl protested. "I don't even know how to go home. Please, can't I stay?"

The old woman stood. "I'll help you find your way, child." She walked to a cupboard, opened it, reached in, and pulled out a gingerbread boy. She handed the gingerbread boy to the girl, saying, "Put this in your pocket. Eat it after you reach home." The girl put the gingerbread boy in her pocket. She was about to speak again, but the old woman raised her hand, and the girl fell silent. "Your life will be better, child," the old woman assured her. "You'll see."

The two of them left the old woman's house. In a very short time, the old woman had led the girl through the woods and within sight of the old wagon. They said their goodbyes. Then the girl retrieved her hoe from under the wagon and trudged on home.

When she walked into the house, she smelled freshly baked bread. Her stepmother sat at the kitchen table, knife in hand, slicing the loaf. When she saw the girl, she set down her knife. "I don't know where you've been, but you were not chopping out the cotton like I told you." As she spoke, she leaned over and picked up the chain beside her chair. "Don't think you'll be eating any of this bread."

When the girl saw the chain, she ran toward her room. Her stepmother came after her, whirling the chain. The girl ducked as she ran into her room. She slammed the door and braced herself against it. She could feel the door shudder as the chain struck it again and again. Finally the stepmother tired and returned to her chair at the table.

The girl braced a chair under the doorknob to keep her stepmother out; then she collapsed on her bed and cried. She cried for her father and mother. She cried in longing for the joy of that afternoon. She cried and cried. When she was cried out, she rolled over and felt the gingerbread boy in her pocket. She took it out, looked at it, held it by the head, and bit off an arm.

Out in the other room, the stepmother sat eating warm bread slathered in butter. Suddenly her knife flew out of her hand and—*whack!*—it cut off her arm. She couldn't scream. She just stared at her arm on the floor.

Back in the bedroom, the girl ate the other arm. *Whack!* The stepmother's other arm landed on the floor.

The girl ate a leg. *Whack!* One leg gone.

The girl ate the other leg. *Whack!* Another leg on the floor.

Then the girl broke off the body from the head. *Whack!* The stepmother's head fell to the floor.

After she finished eating the gingerbread boy, the girl fell asleep.

The next morning, when the girl walked out of her room, she found her stepmother's body in pieces. No blood on the floor— just pieces.

The girl knew just what to do. She took a shovel from the shed, and she dug a grave. She had worked so hard for so many years; she had no trouble digging a hole six feet deep. Of course, she had no need to make it six feet long. After all, the body was in pieces!

In the times that followed, the girl lived on there in her own house. She and the old woman in the woods became fast friends and the very best of neighbors.

Story Notes

I encountered this story in the Leonard Roberts Collection in the Southern Appalachian Archives at Berea College, Berea, Kentucky. Leonard Roberts reported collecting this tale from Billie Jean Fields in Martin County, Kentucky, in 1970 under the title "The Family," and from Margie Day in Leslie County, Kentucky, before 1954 under the title "The Candy Doll." Retold with permission of the Leonard Roberts family and Berea College.

When telling this story, "Whack!" is such fun to say! Audience members may be startled at first. By the time you reach the last Whack! some listeners will look downright gleeful, others will cringe. Enjoy the mix!

MARY HAMILTON, a Frankfort, Kentucky-based storyteller and workshop leader, grew up on a Kentucky farm where telling stories was considered a moral failing. After years of confessing her storytelling sins, she finally gave in to temptation and found her career. Since 1983 Mary has strengthened imaginations from Florida to Alaska with her straightforward, just-talking storytelling style. When she takes the stage, worlds unfold in the hearts and minds of her audience. Learn more about her work at www.maryhamilton.info.

The Mournful Lady of Binnorie

Based on a Scottish Ballad
Bobbie Pell

A long time ago in the north country, where green hills rambled at will and wild heathers purpled the sloping banks beside the surging Binnorie River waters, there lived a king, his queen, and their two lovely daughters. Now, as was proper in the those days, the eldest married first, so Lady Helen, two years senior to her younger sister Isobelle, was betrothed to Sir William, a nobleman from a neighboring county. This arranged union would guarantee power and lands for the two noble families, so Sir William vowed his ring and monogrammed glove to seal the marriage contract.

All seemed well until one day, while confirming wedding plans, Sir William cast his eye upon the lovely Isobelle. She was fair of face, with sapphire blue eyes. Her long golden hair reached down past her waist in thick braids strung with pearls. Everyone who met her claimed Isobelle's gentleness and goodness were matched only by the saints themselves. Her frame was slight and trim, and she cut a fine figure in Sir William's eyes. Immediately he fell in love with her and set out to woo her, to win her, despite his earlier agreement with Lady Helen. The younger princess found herself overwhelmed with affection for this nobleman and could not refuse his advances. The pair met in secret, their lovers' trysts known to no one.

But Sir William, now truly in love, made his own decision. He broke off the engagement with Lady Helen in order to marry Isobelle.

When Lady Helen first heard his declaration, she listened in disbelief. How could he humiliate her like this? Was she not as fair to look upon as her sister? But more than that, was she not the eldest? And although she had not truly loved Sir William, she did think him of fine breeding, good stock for ruling families, and she appreciated his pleasant nature. Despite his wish, the younger sister could not marry until Lady Helen herself was neatly wed. But to be outstripped by her younger sister, to be mocked by the peasants as unfit to be a bride—why, this would not do!

She must concoct a scheme—a wicked, deadly plan.

She hid herself away in her chambers, pacing the velvet carpet until rutted tracks revealed her frustration. "I must think of a way to get rid of her!" she cried aloud, her jealous anger resounding against the castle's stone walls. "But it must be done in such a way that no will ever suspect that I was involved."

When deceitful thoughts enter the heart, ugly actions follow.

She continued to circle until an idea emerged, curling her lips into a cold smile. She sat by the window, gazing past the bottom lands and furrowed fields, across the Binnorie River to the mighty ocean beyond. "I know exactly what to do, and nobody will ever dream I had anything to do with such a tragedy." She popped a chocolate candied mint into her mouth, then licked her lips like a cat after eating its first mouse.

The next morning after breakfast, she stood behind Isobelle's chair and asked, "Shall we not go down to the lovely Binnorie River today and watch as our father's ships come in from sea? I've been told they are laden with jewels for our choosing and some of the finest silks for our dancing gowns. It's such a brilliant day, shall we not go?"

Isobelle agreed without hesitation, so the two set off along the winding river path that led down to the water. As they approached the rippling waves of the Binnorie, Isobelle noticed a large flat stone overlooking the banks. She stepped upon it, gazing out to her father's ships, now visible across the sea.

Lady Helen strode purposefully up behind her sister. Without warning, she grabbed Isobelle by the waist and plunged the young princess into the raging waters of the Binnorie River below, knowing full well the poor girl could not swim.

"Helen, Helen, give me your hand, and I'll give you half of all my lands!" Isobelle struggled with the words, gulping and gasping as her body bobbled in the frothy waters.

But Lady Helen remained still, unmoved by such pleas. She cried out, "I'll not touch a hair on your head—as you lie beneath the waters, completely dead!"

"But Helen, Helen, give me your glove, and I'll give you back William, your own true love!"

Once more Lady Helen stood rigid, determined in her will. "I'll have William and all your lands as you sink beneath the waves to watery hands!" And with that, Lady Helen turned and made her way back to the castle.

Now poor Isobelle floated and sank, floated and sank, until her body simply floated, face down, in the waves.

The river ran to the home of a miller whose stone wheel spun in its work. The miller's daughter had come down to the river for some water for the noonday meal when she saw something upstream coming toward her—a ghostly, gleaming shape. "Father! Father! Stop the wheel! There's a sinking swan or a lonely maiden swimming in distress. Please, Father, stop the wheel!"

The miller did as she bid him, then came running to his daughter's side. The pair watched as the still form of the young princess drew near. The miller stepped into the shallows of the stream and lifted the girl from her watery grave, laying her in the high grasses.

The miller and his daughter stood there, wondering what to do. As they did, a minstrel, a traveling harper, came upon this tragic group. He saw the drowned form of this poor young woman, wearing a white gown that reached her lily white ankles. A golden girdle draped across her chest while gleaming pearls were strewn throughout her long, blonde hair. Her lackluster eyes stared into the blue sky above her. Yet even in death, he thought her to be the loveliest creature he had ever seen. He mused a moment, then left.

The harper continued on his way, but every night for the months that followed, his dreams were disturbed, haunted by that lovely face, the soulless eyes fixed heavenward. He found himself traveling back into that same country, back to that same village, and back to the very spot where he had last seen her lay. Both the miller and his daughter had not known the young woman; and for fear of being blamed with her death, they had told not a soul, so the body had remained in the tall grasses. After the birds of prey had taken their fill, all that remained of the young woman were her bones, now bleached by the sun, and her long blonde hair.

Following a compulsion from somewhere deep within, this harper took her breast bone, broke it, and formed it into a rude harp. He braided three strands of her golden hair, then strung the harp with them. The soothing strains that emanated from beneath his touch could melt a heart of stone. He stood there, holding this strange instrument, and wondered what to do next. Within seconds the answer came to him, as if whispered on the wind. So placing this new harp under one arm and his older harp under the other, he made his way to the castle.

As it happened, there was a feast at the castle, the wedding feast for Lady Helen and Sir William. The family sat at the high table on the royal dais, sipping wine and attempting to make light conversation. Both the king and queen still mourned the loss of their lovely Isobelle and were bewildered by her disappearance. But as weeks dissolved into months with not a word, either good or ill, they turned their affections to their remaining daughter. Lady Helen, for her part, seemed more than pleased with her nuptial success while Sir William looked dutifully upon the festivities.

When the court heard news of the arrival of the harper, an honored musician, they made a space for him where he could regale the party with music and song. He pulled out his old harp and sang songs of romance, of valor, of truth. But then he took the new harp and placed it in the center of the room, where all could see it. In low and mournful tones, the voice of the missing princess, the younger sister, filled the court as the harp itself began to sing.

> He laid the harp upon a stone.
> Bow down, bow down.
> And there it began to play alone.
> Binnorie, oh Binnorie.
> And I'll be true to my true love
> If my love be true to me.

Everyone sat amazed, but the harp continued.

> Oh yonder sits my father, King.
> Bow down, bow down.
> And yonder sits my mother, Queen.
> Binnorie, oh Binnorie.

> And yonder stands my brother Hugh
> And with him my William, sweet and true.
> And I'll be true to my true love
> If my love be true to me.

The family began casting wary glances at one another at this unholy sound. But the harp sang on. The last note sang out sad and low.

> And now at last my tears shall flow.
> Woe to my sister, false Helen,
> Who drowned me for the sake of a man!

As the mournful song came to an end, the harp broke into a thousand pieces.

Lady Helen rose from her chair, staring ahead of her as if the ghostly specter of her sister were floating toward her. She began clutching her throat, scrabbling at invisible, icy fingers taking the very life from her. And before her family could reach her, she fell to the floor—stone cold dead.

So when jealousy makes its way into your heart, beware. For true love always wins, even if it reaches out from the grave.

Story Notes

This story was originally performed as a ballad. Contemporary Celtic singers often seek out traditional tunes (See Dr. Francis Child's The English and Scottish Popular Ballads, *vol. 5, Ballad Airs, "Twa Sisters," p. 411) or create adaptations of their own making. As you tell this story, you may wish to sing the portions that have remained in verse. Remember that a capella singing (without instrumental accompaniment) is also the traditional delivery style. To convey the emotional drama, use the drowning scene to focus on Isobelle's innocence and Lady Helen's betrayal. Remember to read this story with your own inner compass, directing the audience toward your points of connection with the themes presented. Remember that it is a ghost story, so variations with voice pitch and volume will create suspense and serve you well. Enjoy!*

Sources

"The Twa Sisters." [Child Ballad #10:C, Scott's Minstrelsy, 1802).

McKennitt, Lorenna. "The Bonny Swans." The Mask and the Mirror. Burbank, California: Warner Brothers, 1994. Traditional lyrics adapted by Loreena McKennitt.

Jacobs, Joseph. "Binnorie." English Fairy Tales. New York: Dover Publications, 1967 [1890].

BOBBIE PELL, the Moonstone Minstrel, has been telling stories and writing fiction and poetry for more than twenty-five years. A lifelong lover of story, Bobbie incorporates folklore, myth, and faerie lore into her writings, workshops, courses, and storytelling performances. She holds master's degrees in library science, English literature and composition, and creative writing. She lives in western North Carolina and teaches at the University of North Carolina at Asheville and East Tennessee State University.

Ghostly Guardians

The Angel of River Road

Based on a Family Story
Larry G. Brown

*Matilda Wilkening Hageman was my great-grandmother. When
she died, I wasn't allowed to attend her funeral because I was only five
years old. Although so young, I remembered this tiny old lady, ninety-
four years old and my oldest living relative, as a warm and friendly
person who sat in the rocking chair at my Great-Aunt Bessie's home.
She had tight white curls of hair and wore little round spectacles.
Every one called her Tillie.*

*Her family, the Wilkenings, had moved from Prussia to the
United States and settled around Cincinnati, Ohio, after the
American Civil War, as the German Empire was beginning to build.
That history explained why she spoke with a bit of German accent.*

*I was more than disappointed that I couldn't go to the funeral. I
was angry. So when the family came back to Great-Aunt Bessie's
house for a big dinner, I refused to eat. Instead I went out on the front
porch swing and sulked. After a while, my grandmother, one of Tillie's
daughters, came to sit with me and told me this story.*

In the 1880s, as a young woman, Tillie went to work in a
clothing factory as a seamstress. Today we would probably call
that factory a "sweatshop." Tillie was good at her job and was
promoted to supervisor. At this time electric lights were just
coming into use, and that meant Tillie would often have to stay
late at the factory to organize work for the next day.

Typically, all the young women working at the factory lived in boardinghouses a few blocks down the street from the factory, along what was called River Road. This was the industrial, warehouse, and shipping district of Cincinnati, on the banks of the Ohio River. The young women would walk together at the end of each day to get to the boardinghouses. A boardwalk ran along the edge of River Road, a street that was often muddy but still the business center of the district. For safety, the women traveled in groups past all the hustle and bustle of the taverns and shops.

Tillie had to walk those few blocks to her boardinghouse alone when her work required her to stay late at the factory. She found the boardwalk too noisy, crowded, and dangerous to walk comfortably and the horse and wagon traffic of the street no less hazardous; eventually she decided that the safest place to walk was at the outer edge of the boardwalk next to the street.

One night, as Tillie walked home, she passed a loud and boisterous brawl in front of one of the taverns. Tillie stepped into the street to avoid the fighting, but there she had to dodge the traffic. When Tillie finally arrived at the steps of her boardinghouse, her roommate Sally came bounding down the steps to greet her with a series of questions.

"Oh Tillie, oh Tillie, who is that handsome man I saw escorting you through the crowd?" Sally asked. "Is he your new beau?"

"What do you mean?" Tillie snapped back. "I was not with any man!"

"OK, Tillie, you don't have to tell me. You can just keep your little secret," Sally teased.

"That's not funny!" Tillie brushed past Sally. Sally kept quiet.

☠☠☠

A few weeks later, Tillie was again making her way home in the evening, through the crowds along River Road. Again she had to pass a loud and angry brawl involving two men, one of whom had been forced into the street by the other, who was brandishing a knife. Tillie stopped. The man withdrew his knife, and the crowd let her pass by.

When Tillie opened the door to the boardinghouse, Sally was standing just inside. "Oh Tillie, I saw it all from our window! Your beau is so brave! I saw him pull out his gun and make that man with the knife back away. You must be so proud!" Sally said excitedly.

"Sally, this is no time to be teasing me. That was a very dangerous episode. I don't know why the man with the knife backed away, but there was no man with a gun. There is no beau." Tillie was obviously upset.

"But Tillie," Sally insisted, "I saw him."

"That's enough, Sally. No more!" Tillie went to their room. Sally followed silently and resolved not to bring the subject up again.

☠☠☠

A few days later, on a Sunday afternoon, Tillie and Sally were cleaning up around the boardinghouse and had carried out some trash and papers to the backyard to burn. Suddenly Sally reached down into the burn pile and pulled out a smoldering newspaper. Hastily she put out the flames.

"It's him! It's him!" Sally shouted. "It's your beau, Tillie!"

"What on earth are you talking about?" Tillie grabbed the paper and Sally leaned over her shoulder pointing. "See the picture? It's him!"

That page of the newspaper featured an artist's hand-drawn rendering of what might have been a tintype photograph of a young man in a uniform. His name was Robert McKelvie. But to the women's surprise, they discovered they were reading an obituary in a newspaper that was several months old.

"I don't understand, Tillie. That's the man I saw escorting you through the crowd a few days ago," Sally declared.

The women looked at each other blankly for a moment and then went back to reading the yellowed, charred newspaper. Robert McKelvie had been a guard at one of the factories on River Road and had been killed while attempting to rescue some women from a fracas outside one of the taverns. Tillie and Sally could not believe what they were reading. There was an address given in the article, and Tillie swore they would get to the bottom of this mystery.

☠☠☠

The next Sunday afternoon, Tillie and Sally took a streetcar to a distant part of Cincinnati, a neighborhood they had never visited before. They found the address to be occupied by a little house on a tree-lined street. A tiny elderly lady answered their knock on the door and invited them to sit in the parlor while she made tea.

"I suppose you are here about my Robert," she said.

Tillie and Sally looked at each other and back toward the woman. "Yes ..." Sally said with some hesitation.

"I know," the old lady said quietly. "You two are not the first, and I suppose you will not be the last. So many have told me that after my son was killed, they have seen him helping young women down the street through that awful district. You know that they have been calling him the angel of River Road?"

She went on to explain that Robert was always so distressed that he could not do anything to make that street safer, but he couldn't leave his post. "That one night he did try to help, and that was the night he was killed," she finished.

Tillie and Sally stayed and chatted a while with Mrs. McKelvie. They thanked her for telling them about Robert and for her hospitality.

☠☠☠

Tillie walked with confidence down River Road from then on. There were still nights when she had to make her way through the foreboding chaos of the boardwalk and the street.

But when she reached the steps of her boardinghouse, she could always pause and look back a couple of blocks in time to see a man in uniform waving to her.

Story Notes

This story gives the teller the opportunity to share both narrative and dialogue. When I tell the story I vocalize Tillie as stern and assertive, while Sally is teasing and Mrs. McKelvie is quiet and gentle. There are plenty of opportunities in the story to physically suggest objects such as the knife, the gun, the newspaper, to point directions, or indicate a wave. I encourage tellers to visualize the setting for themselves and utilize posture, tone, volume, and tempo to invite the audience to share your visualization. This is a good complement to a study of the conditions of female industrial laborers in the late nineteenth century.

DR. LARRY G. BROWN is an Assistant Professor of Geography at the University of Missouri–Columbia. He has been an active storyteller for more than twenty-five years; he was co-founder and is current co-president of the Mid-Missouri Organization for Storytelling (MOST) and is president of the National Storytelling Network's special interest group, Storytelling in Higher Education. He tells to all ages and is known for his original Ozark Jack tales, humorous chicken sagas, and mystery stories; he is a frequent teller at storytelling festivals in the Midwest. Although a native of Nebraska, he has returned to his family's heritage in the Ozarks and has been a resident of Missouri since 1975.

One Lace Glove

A Civil War Ghost Story
Lorna MacDonald Czarnota

I suppose it is time to tell of that strange night outside Gettysburg in July 1863. The federal army had come from all over the place, some of us marching back north through the Cumberland Gap and already looking sorely defeated—but not willing to give up the capital to the Confederacy. I think most of us knew if we lost this battle we could outright lose the war and our families up north would never forgive us. It's not really a time I like to remember in my waking hours as it still haunts my sleep, but I suspect it has to be told sooner or later.

The first day was a complete loss for us, as it turned out, and the second was only somewhat better. The Union army, dazed by defeat, was trying desperately to recover from the previous day's battle.

There was no telling how long I'd been lying in that spot beneath the outcropping of boulders. I only knew that the sun had been hot and now the stars shone overhead. My only recollection was of cannon fire, fragments of rock flying in every direction, the sulfurous acrid smell of gunpowder, and a flash of light just behind my eyes.

Now, as my eyes adjusted to the darkness, I took stock of my surroundings. My head thundered, and the blood still trickled from behind my ear. It hadn't been too long, I thought, or it would have dried by now. I felt around for my rifle. Gone.

No surprise. They take everything they find after a battle, even a man's boots. I looked. I still had my shoes at least. I untied my bandana and wrapped it around my head, which was throbbing with pain. The bandage was soon soaked with blood, but I had worse problems than that. I was separated from my regiment.

The moon was shrouded in a cloud, more of gunpowder than rain. I wondered, did the Rebs take the hill? Did they get the wheat field and the peach orchard too? Had we lost so much for so little? Could I even dare to move without being spotted? Was I among friend or foe? I had to move, but I also had to keep low, so I crawled on hands and knees. Keeping my head down made it hurt all the more.

The battlefield was a gruesome sight. In the glow cast by the cloud-shadowed moon, I could make out dark lumps on the ground—the dead and dying. I knew instinctively they were both Union and Reb. When a man bleeds, the blood is red. It doesn't matter where he comes from or what he believes. I learned that one thing: dead is dead.

I listened for the sounds of a normal night: singing in the distance, a cough, a whisper, the crackle of a campfire. All around me I heard the hideous cries of wounded men—but one in particular caught my ear, as it was unmistakably a soldier's desperate gasp. I tilted my head. The cry came from the east, according to the stars. It was a moan, close by, a deep long lonesome desperate moan.

Maybe I could help. I'd killed so many by the light of day, I'd seen them go down, I'd shouted "Hoorah!" But now in the night, when a gray uniform looks so much like a blue one, maybe I could help.

One by one, blurred faces came into view. No color, only faces. Then I saw him—a young man lying on his back with a great hole in his chest and his life's blood soaking into the ground beneath him. I knew before I reached his side that there was nothing to do for him but to lend him comfort. He sensed my presence.

"Water," he whispered.

I still had my canteen, if only because it was slung across my shoulder. Carefully I lifted the young man's head into my lap.

"Just a little, lad," I said. "It'll be all right." Hadn't I seen my colonel aid many a fallen boy in just such a way? Now I had my own piece of work to do, and so I did it.

He looked at me with such a blank stare. "Mary Sue."

"Quiet, lad. Try to rest," I said.

"Mary Sue," he repeated.

When I wiped his face with my sleeve, I noticed that he wasn't looking at me when he spoke. He was looking past me, over my shoulder. I turned and was startled to see the prettiest girl I'd ever seen. But I would have jumped out of my skin had I not been held with the lad's head in my lap. Where her eyes should have been there were only two black holes!

"Mary Sue," he said again.

"Mary Sue?" I repeated.

The girl raised her arm, and the sleeve of her white party dress moved in the light breeze. Her hair fell in ringlets over her shoulders, and on her raised hand she wore a white lace glove. Her other hand hung bare at her side.

I gaped as she moved closer. I could not see her feet. She floated just inches above the ground. I felt a scream rise up in the back of my throat, but it stuck there and nothing came out. It seemed like the earth and the weight of the young man were holding me down, pinning me so I could not move. My head ached. *This is a serious wound I have*, I thought to myself. It had to be the wound. Had to be. I tried to make sense of it.

She was so close now I heard the rustle of her skirts. I smelled her perfume. And this I swear to you now on my father's own good name: while I was still holding that young man in my arms, I saw him stand and take the girl's gloved hand in his.

That was the first time I saw his colors. They were gray, the colors of the Confederacy. But the hole in his chest was gone, his uniform was clean and pressed, the buttons glistened in the moonlight. And yet, I could look down into his face right there in my lap and see him smiling up at me. His spirit—or whatever it was—took her hand and laid it over his arm, and the two of them rose and floated west toward the Blue Ridge Mountains.

My throat ached. My head pounded as my heart beat faster, and a tear fell to my cheek. I watched as they moved farther and farther away. All of a sudden, she turned back. She left him standing there and came back to lean over me. I felt the pressure of her hand on my shoulder. I turned my head, and from the corner of my eye I saw the white glove on that hand.

"My William and I thank you for your kindness, sir."

I sat frozen. I didn't know what to say or what to do as she returned to him and the two of them vanished right before my eyes. They melted just like the waking memories of that night have melted for me until now.

But truth be told, I will never forget them. For you see, I still have her other glove. I found it stuffed between the buttons in that dead soldier's jacket. It is stained red but it smells as sweet as magnolia perfume. And you see, I have learned that dead isn't always dead.

Story Notes

The Battle of Gettysburg in 1863 is considered the bloodiest battle fought on American soil. At the end of three days of fighting, fifty thousand men, five thousand horses, and at least one woman lay dead in the hot July sun. Every person and every place in the small nearby town were touched by the stench of death. The battlefield, now a national memorial, is thought to be one of the most haunted places in the United States. Stand on Cemetery Ridge in the dark and you can feel the hairs on the back of your neck stand on end. Telling ghost stories is like that feeling. Tell them like you were there, like you saw it, like you felt it.

Storyteller LORNA MACDONALD CZARNOTA is the author of *Medieval Tales That Kids Can Read and Tell*. She has delighted audiences in schools, libraries, festivals, and conferences throughout the U.S., Canada, and Ireland with traditional and original stories for more than twenty years. Her work features historical presentations on the American Civil War, the Middle Ages, the Dust Bowl, and Colonial America. Lorna specializes in storytelling to at-risk youth, therapeutic narrative, Celtic folklore, and the use of music to enhance story. She lives in Buffalo, New York.

The Boy Who Drew Cats

A Japanese Folktale
Judy Sima

In ancient Japan lived a poor farmer and his wife. They had many children. The youngest son's name was Sesshu. Every day Sesshu and his family went to work in the rice paddies. Although he was small and weak, little Sesshu worked beside his parents, brothers, and sisters. But as often as not, you could see him drawing in the dirt, for that is what he liked to do most of all.

Sesshu drew the snow-capped mountains. He drew the flowers, birds, and trees. He drew his family working in the rice paddies. But, what he liked to draw most of all, were cats.

Cats, Cats, Cats.
Cats eating, sleeping, jumping, leaping,
Cats, Cats, Cats.
Cats fighting, biting, howling, yowling,
Cats, Cats, Cats.

When times were good, Sesshu's parents bought him fine white rice paper. Once, when the rice harvest was especially bountiful, they bought him a bamboo brush with fine horsehair bristles, a round stone hollowed out in the middle, and a stick of shiny black ink. He ground the ink stick into the ink stone and mixed it with a little water. Dipping the brush into the ink, he drew his beloved cats.

One year, however, there was a terrible famine upon the land. It was said a huge Rat Goblin held a spell over all of Japan. In winter it opened its greedy mouth and swallowed snowflakes. When the rains came, it lapped up the drops of water. When the rice began to grow, the terrible rat gnawed on the tender seedlings and the rice stalks withered and died. The harvest was poor, and people went to bed hungry.

With very little food to feed their family, Sesshu's parents worried that their young son would not live through the winter. So they decided to take him to the next village, where there was a temple. Perhaps the priests would take him in, take care of him, and teach him to be a priest. They wrapped Sesshu's few belongings in a blanket and set out for the temple, and when they arrived, Sesshu's father knocked on the door. As the paper screen door slid aside, an old priest greeted them. Sesshu's parents bowed to him.

"There is a famine in the land. We are poor farmers and cannot feed our family. Our youngest son is small and frail. We are afraid he will not live though the winter. Please take him in and teach him to be a priest. He is a good boy and will do whatever you ask."

The old priest asked Sesshu a few questions. When the boy answered his questions quickly and accurately, the priest saw that Sesshu was a bright child and agreed to take him in. Sesshu bowed to his parents and bid them farewell. He followed the priest to a small room where he unrolled his blanket and put away his few belongings. Underneath the blanket, he hid his prize possessions—his bamboo brush, ink stick, and mixing stone. Then he followed the old priest into the temple.

"You will have to work hard, Sesshu," said the old priest. "You must keep the temple floors clean and work in the rice paddies. And when the priests pray at night, you must pray with us."

Sesshu promised to work hard, and indeed he did. He worked so hard at his tasks that he went to bed exhausted each night, and for many weeks he did not think once about drawing. So it was a surprise to Sesshu when, early one morning while the priests were still sleeping, he woke up with an uncontrollable urge to draw. He took out his ink stick and chipped some ink onto the mixing stone. Then he took a little water, mixed it together with the bamboo brush, and began to draw ... all over the temple floors! What did he draw?

> Cats, Cats, Cats.
> Cats eating, sleeping, jumping, leaping,
> Cats, Cats, Cats.
> Cats fighting, biting, howling, yowling,
> Cats, Cats, Cats.

When the priests came into the temple and saw the cats, they said, "Who did this? This should not be!" But Sesshu said nothing.

Weeks passed, and Sesshu worked hard, keeping the temple floors clean, working in the rice paddies, and going to prayers. But again, he woke up very early one morning and had a terrible urge to draw. He took out his ink stick, his mixing stone, and his bamboo brush. He added water to the ink, mixed it together, and began to draw all over the temple walls. And what did he draw?

> Cats, Cats, Cats.
> Cats eating, sleeping, jumping, leaping,
> Cats, Cats, Cats.
> Cats fighting, biting, howling, yowling,
> Cats, Cats, Cats.

Once again, when the priests came into the temple and looked upon the walls they said, "Who did this? This must not be." But again Sesshu said nothing.

Many more weeks passed before Sesshu woke again with that urge to draw. He took out his ink stick, mixing stone, and brush. This time when the priests awoke, they did not notice anything unusual. Sesshu swept the temple floors and worked in the rice paddies. That night, when the priest opened their books to pray, what did they see?

Cats, Cats, Cats.
Cats eating, sleeping, jumping, leaping,
Cats, Cats, Cats.
Cats fighting, biting, howling, yowling,
Cats, Cats, Cats.

The old priest looked at Sesshu and said, "Is it you who have drawn on our floors, walls, and prayer books?"

Sesshu hung his head and said, "Yes, it was I."

"Sesshu, it is obvious that you were meant to be an artist, not a priest. You must leave. But before you go, I will give you some advice. Avoid large places at night. Stay to small spaces."

Sesshu thanked the old priest. Then, taking his belongings and blanket, he left the temple.

The Rat Goblin still held Japan in its spell. There would not be enough food in his parents' village, so Sesshu walked toward the nearest village in the opposite direction. "Perhaps there is a temple. If I work hard and do not draw, maybe they will let me stay."

He walked until he came to the next village. Like Sesshu's village, the people were also affected by the drought. Here, too, the Rat Goblin's spell kept the rains from falling and the rice from growing.

Sesshu stopped everyone he met. "Can you tell me where I might find the temple?"

The people's faces were pinched with worry and hunger. They scurried away and did not answer.

Finally, he asked a gnarled old woman, "Please, tell me where I might find the temple."

She pointed to a steep hill just outside the village. Sesshu bowed, thanked the old woman, and started to turn away, but she touched his arm and warned, "Avoid large places at night. Stay to small spaces."

It took the entire day, but he finally reached the top of the hill. The temple grounds were littered with leaves and dirt. Sesshu thought to himself, *I will sweep the grounds clean.* As he knocked on the old door frame, he noticed the wood was cracked and the paper door was torn. *I will fix the door. I will work very hard, and maybe they will let me stay.*

When no one answered, he carefully slid the door aside and walked into the temple. It seemed to be deserted. Sesshu was very tired after his long walk, so he rolled out his blanket and lay down. As he closed his eyes, he noticed several large pure white rice-paper screens on the far wall. Sesshu sat up. They were beautiful!

Seeing the screens, Sesshu again had an uncontrollable urge to draw. He took out his ink stick and chipped some ink into the mixing stone. Then he took a little water from the courtyard, mixed it together with the bamboo brush, and began to draw. What did he draw?

Cats, Cats, Cats.
Cats eating, sleeping, jumping, leaping,
Cats, Cats, Cats.
Cats fighting, biting, howling, yowling,
Cats, Cats, Cats.

Never had Sesshu drawn such beautiful cats. They were almost perfect. Lying down again, he closed his eyes. Then he remembered the words of the old priest and the old woman, *Avoid large places at night. Stay to small spaces.* Though the temple was itself huge, on one side of the room he found a small cupboard just big enough for a small boy and a blanket. Sesshu squeezed himself in and fell asleep.

Around midnight, Sesshu woke to a loud scratching and sniffing. He was so frightened that he could scarcely breathe. The scratching and sniffing came closer and closer. It stopped right at the cupboard door. *Scraaatch, scraaatch, scraaatch. Sniff, sniff, sniff.*

Then, to his astonishment, one long black claw pierced the cupboard wall.

"EEEEYOWWW!"

Sesshu heard a tremendous growling and hissing, followed by a horrible screeching and screaming, thrashing and dashing. The boy covered his ears, but he could still hear tearing and ripping, roaring and bumping. All night long the terrible sounds continued. Just before dawn, it grew deathly quiet.

Sesshu waited until the first rays of sunlight filtered through the cupboard door. Then, very cautiously, he opened the door and peeked outside. In the middle of the floor lay an enormous rat. It was as big as a cow. Its bones were broken, and its flesh was torn apart. There was blood all over the floor, and the rat lay still, as silent as death.

"Who saved me? Who killed the Rat Goblin?" Sesshu looked around.

There, on the rice-paper screens, from the mouths of each of the cats he had drawn the night before, dripped blood and rat's flesh. During the night, the cats had come alive and saved Sesshu's life.

Sesshu bowed to the cats, then rolled up his blanket and left the temple. Outside, a light rain was falling. Now that the Rat Goblin was dead and the spell was broken, rice would grow again. Sesshu walked toward his own village. When he arrived, his family was overjoyed to see him.

They say that Sesshu lived a long and happy life in the village. Indeed, he became a famous artist. To this very day, people in Japan admire his paintings. Sesshu drew the snow-capped mountains. He drew the flowers, birds, and trees. He drew the people working in the rice paddies. But every day, no matter what, he was always sure to draw at least one or two cats!

Cats, Cats, Cats.
Cats eating, sleeping, jumping, leaping,
Cats, Cats, Cats.
Cats fighting, biting, howling, yowling,
Cats, Cats, Cats.

Story Notes

My version of this Japanese story was adapted from a text originally published in 1918 by Lafcadio Hearn, an American writer who lived in Japan and collected many traditional Japanese tales.

"The Boy Who Drew Cats" is based on a legend about a fifteenth-century artist, Sesshu Toyo, whose ink drawings were said to be so realistic that they would sometimes come to life. Ever since I began my storytelling career by telling scary stories in the library of my elementary and middle-school students it has been one of our favorites.

In telling the story I try to create spooky and gory images using my voice, facial expressions, and body. When repeating the refrain— "Cats. Cats. Cats"—I emphasize each word as if I were reciting a poem. At the same time, I move my hands to the rhythm and imitate a cat crawling, jumping, fighting, and leaping higher and higher.

It's always fun if I can make my audience jump at the most suspenseful part. When I come to the scene where Sesshu is hiding in the cupboard and the scratching and sniffing sounds are drawing closer, I lower my voice and look down at the floor. Then I look up at the audience while screeching—"EEEEYOWWW!"—and throwing my hands into the air. It works every time!

Storyteller, author, and educator, JUDY SIMA loves to tell scary stories! As a performer and workshop leader, she has appeared across the country. In her thirty-five-year career as a school librarian, she introduced many young people to the art of storytelling through her middle-grade storytelling troupe. Her book, *Raising Voices: Creating Youth Storytelling Groups and Troupes*, has received numerous awards and accolades. Her articles on storytelling have been featured in educational and storytelling journals too numerous to mention. Judy lives in Detroit, but you can visit her online at www.JudySima.com.

The Greyman of Pawleys Island

Based on Maritime Legend
Timothy E. Dillinger

Many spirits have inhabited the waterways over the years. Men have gone near and men have gone far, but the one thing, the one thread that holds them all together is the fear of great storms. Winds that blow—*whooooo*—can take a man's life. And sometimes they need a patron saint, someone to give them warning, because even old mariners don't always know what the weather is going to do.

This is a story about a man who is our shadowy figure, our patron saint of Pawleys Island, South Carolina. A spirit that we call the *Greyman*. Now, the story is he was the son of a rice plantation owner; he could have had whatever he wanted, as he was raised in a time and place of utter affluence.

Now in the old days, the rice culture was so strong that a man never really had to work because all the hard work had already been done. This young man's family plantation boasted thousands of acres and slaves in the fields, and the days went by slowly. The young man decided that he couldn't stand the tedium of being at home any more. Being the son of privilege, he could have had anything he wanted, but he liked the simple life of a sailing man. The few adventures that were left in the world were to be found at sea. He could make his own fame and fortune on the waterways, not that of his father, and then return home.

This is the young man's story. He got on a ship in Georgetown, South Carolina, and headed off to ports unknown. The winds would blow, and the waves would crash over the bow. Each day was a new adventure.

It was soon apparent to his shipmates that he had an uncanny sixth sense of the weather. He would look across the horizon and see the clouds start to grow dark a long way off. He'd mention to one of the men, "I believe it's going to blow up a gale tonight. We might want to batten down the hatches." That night—*whoosh*—the waves began to crash, the winds started to blow, and the rain came pelting down.

After a while, one or two would start to say, "Yuh, you know the navigator, he seems to know a lot about the weather, doesn't he?"

"Oh yeah, he's never been wrong."

The other sailors put great stock in what the man had to say. Quickly he worked his way up through the hierarchy of the ship until he was entrusted with the charts. Now he was the most valued member of the crew: you never throw your navigator overboard; he may be the only man who can get you home.

In time the young man grew tired of his life on the sea. He had traveled far and wide and seen many wondrous sights, but he began to long for his family back home, and his thoughts often turned to the young lady he had once courted. He decided it was time to come home.

Our seafarer arrived in the Port of Charleston and sent word ahead that he had returned and was hoping to find his family well and to see the plantation once again. He also sent a second message to the young lady he had begun to miss more each day. He knew that one day he would probably ask for her hand. He sent a message ahead, knowing there would be a grand party, a reception in his honor. He would be thrilled to meet his old friends.

So he went back to Pawleys Island. He returned to a grand party, a reception in his honor. As his father said, "Ah, I couldn't be happier if I tried in me life." The seafarer was thrilled to see his old friends but most of all to see that his childhood sweetheart had blossomed into a lovely young woman. So the courtship rekindled and the engagement was set.

After all those years at sea the man had lost whatever equestrian skills he acquired as a child and began to take daily rides with his manservant. While the young man had forgotten some of his riding skills, his servant on the other hand had improved his, as he was the one who took the messages and the post from plantation to plantation.

Well, the day of the wedding arrived. On this day they decided that they were going to take the shortcut and ride their stallions down the beach as they'd done in their younger days. The two of them started to ride together, and then they started to race. *Clop. Clop. Clop. Clop.*

The two horses are riding side by side—*Clop. Clop. Clop. Clop*—and the men are laughing and yelling back and forth. Just as they start to ride faster and faster and faster, the servant begins to pull ahead.

"Ride on, ride on," says the master. *Clop. Clop. Clop. Clop.* And they keep racing on. The gap between the riders grows farther and farther and farther apart. At the moment when the master knows that he is surely going to lose the race, he decides to try another little trick.

He dashes with all he has. *Clop. Clop. Clop. Clop.* He rides over the dunes to the other side, knowing that Pawleys Island is surrounded by water—the creek side and the sea. Well, the servant—*Clop. Clop. Clop. Clop*—races headlong down the beach. The master now cuts down another path, along the edge of the marsh. He thinks about how the servant will be surprised when he reappears at the end and triumphantly wins the race.

The master races at top speed. *Clop. Clop. Clop. Clop.* The horse leaps over the fallen logs. The master looks up to see an especially wide log in front of him and knows this is going to be a big jump. He leaps and pulls the horse back and comes down to the other side. Much to his shock and surprise, the creek has changed over the years. What used to be solid sand covered with soft grass has been replaced with that stinking black-oyster mud that will suck a man right down like quicksand. The horse can find no landing spot and starts to pull back. The man wants to lean farther on, and the two now tumble end over end, headlong into the sharp oyster bed, strewn with razors of the oyster shells that are down in the black, black mud.

Horse and rider, thrashing, try to separate. The horse with its four big hooves is pounding down on the master, who is now throbbing with pain and not sure which way to go. The man reaches as now the horse desperately pulls itself out and shakes the mud off. The man now finds himself hopelessly trapped. He cries out—"Help! Help me!" —his voice falling off in the open air, muffled by the crashing ocean waves.

Meanwhile—*Clop. Clop. Clop. Clop*—the servant races on. Well, he knows he is winning the race, but he doesn't know by how much, so he looks back over his shoulder hoping to find his master only close at his heels. But much to his shock and surprise, there is nothing but a long set of single tracks in the sand all the way down the beach.

Whoa. He pulls the reins and turns his horse around, and there is nothing on the horizon, no houses, no people—and no master. He has way overextended his courtesies with him and he must go back. *Clop. Clop. Clop. Clop.* He takes off with the horse. *Clop. Clop. Clop. Clop.* He races frantically up the beach until he finally finds where the tracks have split. He turns his horse and takes off and over the dunes again and ... *Clop. Clop. Clop. Clop* ... he hears now the faint cries: "Help me. Help me."

He gets closer and closer. He sees the horse without its rider walking along the beach, covered with mud. He feels a deep sense of dread and races toward the shore. There he finds his master, neck-deep in the mud. He makes a valiant effort, grabbing his own reins and throwing them out as far in the mud as he can. "Grab on!" he beseeches. "Grab on."

To make a long painful story short, his master drowns. He dies as he sinks below the surface. In the marsh mud he is gone.

Now the servant knows he is in very desperate straits. Not only has he lost his master, but he must now be the bearer of bad tidings. He has no choice but to go back to the plantation, where the wedding guests are gathered, and inform his master of the terrible news. He slowly makes his way on. He comes to the plantation house and hears music drifting into the evening air. Sheepishly, he knocks at the door.

"What do you want, boy?" the butler asks.

"My master will not be home this evening."

"What's the matter, boy? What's going on? Speak up."

"My master has fallen from his horse. He's had a terrible accident, and I believe he's drowned."

"What! You didn't kill him, boy? Did yuh?"

"No, no, I didn't kill him, and I really didn't even witness his fall. He, he, tripped and fell in the mud. And I tried. I really tried, and now he's gone. And I'm very sorry. I have to go see if I can find a way to get him back home. Goodbye."

You can imagine how the news goes across the party—like a wave of black death. People who had been happy and jovial moments before now cry and weep. The young lady who was to be married that night is so distraught the only way she can find solace is to go out to the beach, the place that she knows best, where she and her former beau had once walked those many years ago.

As her parents frantically say their goodbyes, she walks out to the beach and looks out to the mist, strangely gathering along the waterfront. As her eyes start to train on the fog, she sees what she believes to be the shadowy figure of a man, walking alone with a long cloak and black, mud-covered riding boots. In his hand, he carries a lantern, lit to guide his way. On his head he wears a dark tricorner hat. He is coming her way, but she realizes that he is moving at a rate much faster than a normal man should go. Where he was way off in the distance only a moment ago, suddenly he appears quite close.

He tips his hat back, and she begins to study his face. She recognizes the features of her former beau, the man she had once loved, the man to whom she had promised her hand in marriage. Now they are standing looking face to face.

Suddenly, she feels this is some form of cruel joke. She raises her hand to strike him, "to slap the taste right out of his mouth," as her mother used to say. Like the mist of the fog, at that very moment—*whoooosh*—he disappears into the night. It is as if he was never really there at all. Well, if the young woman was not already far gone, at this point she is very near the edge and nearly faints from shock.

The young woman rushes back to the plantation house to tell her father what she has just seen. By now, most of the guests are gone. She cries out, "He was there, he was there. I saw him! Father, he was there!" A family friend, a doctor, is brought in to give the young woman something to help her sleep.

That night, in her slumber, she has a strange dream. She sees that shadowy figure of a man even more vividly than she had earlier that evening. She relives the wonderful times that they had had. Throughout this dream, they laugh as in days of old, but she can feel that he is trying to give her a message—that something very, very bad is about to happen and that, at all costs, she and her family must go away from the beach as soon as possible.

In the early morning, she rises and tells her father of the dream she had the night before. He realizes she is still very much struck with grief, so he feels it best to take the family away for a while. They load their belongings and head down the King's Highway south toward Charleston.

The journey takes that entire day and well into the next. As they travel, the skies begin to get very, very dark. The leaves of the trees start to turn belly up. The winds began to blow—*whooooo*—When the rain starts to fall sideways, it's too late to go back. They are already well on their journey. And so they continue on in spite of the approaching storm. They arrive at safety very late the second night—*whooooo*—By now, the winds have increased to the point that trees are falling and roofs are blowing off their houses. Small animals are uprooted from their nests. This is going to be a terrible storm, maybe one of the worst ever recorded up until that time.

That night, at 12:01 A.M. on September 27, 1822, the Great Hurricane struck. When the winds stopped blowing and all was told, more than three hundred people had lost their lives in the middle of the night, all without a clue of what had changed their fate. Many were literally slapped right out of their beds and thrown into the waterways of the Winyah Bay, the Waccamaw, the Black and the Great Pee Dee Rivers, sunken down to the very bottom and never seen or heard from again, their bodies lost to the rolling waves.

But the family has somehow arrived safely in the "holy city" of Charleston, South Carolina. As is often said of the nature of hurricanes, "If it can be in the road, it will be." Or "If it can blow down, it better be tied down." Back home, the next morning, everything along Pawleys Island is topsy-turvy and in disarray. All that can be found is total devastation.

After several weeks in Charleston, the family resolves to go home, fearful of what they will find. On their journey, they see broken houses and bent lives that have been changed forever. There are many wounds to heal. As they approach their own plantation, their hearts begin to sink; total devastation is the only thing to expect. Oddly, though, they begin to notice, not only do the trees along the approach appear to be fuller, but very few limbs or branches litter the landscape.

Slowly and cautiously, they continue down the long oak alley until they get closer and closer to their house. Far off in the distance, they can see the white pillared columns. On examination, they see that not only has their house been spared but several simple things remain unharmed. In their haste, they had failed to secure most of the belongings they had left behind, or even to close the windows.

The shutters gape wide open. Much to the surprise of the family, not a single pane of glass appears broken or even cracked. The maid had run off in such a hurry that clothing still hangs on the line. There is not a single wrinkle in any of those garments. The most amazing thing of all, a simple old, rugged blanket that had been used out on the beach for many years had been laid out casually over the porch railing on the beach side, where it still remains. It should have been moved by the slightest puff of wind, let alone a hurricane of this magnitude. This fact remains a mystery to this very day.

So the legend formed and still remains of this shadowy figure of a man who appears to someone prior to every single hurricane that has struck the Carolinas since the Great Hurricane of 1822. I myself feel I may have met the Greyman at one point in time, before Hurricane Hugo now nearly twenty years ago. But if you see this shadowy figure of a man somewhere along the Grand Strand, be not afraid, because as I (and many others) say, "He is a *good* ghost—not a *bad* ghost." He is there to warn the many visitors and locals alike that hurricanes are on the horizon, even though he speaks not a single word.

If you heed his warning, you can leave in good conscience knowing your life, property, and your mortal soul may have been spared, thankful that a guardian has your best interest at heart.

Keep a watchful eye out for him while you are enjoying your stay at the beach ... for he is always there and will remain watching and waiting for many years to come

And so is the legend of the Greyman of Pawleys Island.

$tory Notes

This is a timeless tale of a shadowy figure seen on the wind-weathered dunes of South Carolina's—and America's—oldest resort. The ghostly spirit of the Greyman has appeared to only a rare few. But accounts of this patron guardian standing, as a sentinel with lantern in hand, have been told again and again by locals to visitors of this historic Grand Strand.

This narrative recounts the part of the legend that few remember: the passage of how the Greyman came to his untimely death and the love he showed to his beloved even after the bitter end. The Greyman's devotion to his fiancé and to the island is most palpable on the eve of a hurricane as a storm rolls up from the rising sea and the wind blows sideways into a raging gale. He appears for only an instant to calm onlookers' fears. If you follow the advice to flee, you can go with a good conscience, for he will steadfastly watch all that you have entrusted him to protect until your safe return.

CAPTAIN TIMOTHY E. DILLINGER lived on Pawleys Island during the storm of Hurricane Hugo in 1989. His personal experiences during the storm and its aftermath inspired him to learn more about the "ghosts of the coast." He has often portrayed the Greyman and many other low-country characters while working as a professional storyteller and artist-in-residence. He now resides in Wilmington, North Carolina, where he has written and illustrated his first children's book. You can find out more at www.captaintimdillinger.com.

Dark Humor

Simon and the Magic Catfish

A Folktale from the Southern United States
Nat Whitman

Once upon a time
there was a little boy named Simon.
Every day, when he was walking to school with his friends
he would peel out from that group ...
and go down by the old muddy river where he had hidden a
fishing pole behind a tree.
Well ... what he would do was he would take this pole
and he would cast out into the brown water and
he would go FISHING ... while all of his friends were in school!

One day he was sitting back and fishing when he got a bite.
And it was a BIG bite!
And he reeled ... and he reeled ... and he held up the line ...
and at the end of the line was a big brown wriggling CATFISH!

That catfish looked Simon in the eye and said,

"Si-i-i-i-mon ... Si-i-i-i-mon ...
Take me home, Simon! Take me home, Simon!
'Cause a catfish wanna go home! Yeah yeah yeah!
A catfish wanna go home! Yeah yeah yeah!"

"Ahhh!" Simon didn't know what to do!
He had a talking catfish bossing him around!
Well, he decided he'd better follow its directions.
So he put that fish into a basket by his side
and he went off to his house.
When he got to the front door of his house
that catfish jumped out of that little basket by Simon's side,
looked him in the eye and said,

"Si-i-i-i-mon ... Si-i-i-i-mon ...
Take me inside, Simon! Take me inside, Simon!
'Cause a catfish wanna go home! Yeah yeah yeah!
A catfish wanna go home! Yeah yeah yeah!"

"Ooooohhhh, okay," said Simon,
and he opened up the door to his house and he walked inside.
And you know what happened next?

"Si-i-i-i-mon ... Si-i-i-i-mon ..."
That catfish was wriggling all around in his basket.
"Take me to the kitchen, Simon! Take me to the kitchen, Simon!
'Cause a catfish wanna go home! Yeah yeah yeah!
A catfish wanna go home! Yeah yeah yeah!"

"Okay." Simon took that catfish to the kitchen.
Then that catfish flopped down on the counter ...
and spun itself around ...
and looked Simon in the eye. It said,

"Si-i-i-i-mon ... Si-i-i-i-mon ...
Cut me up, Simon! Cut me up, Simon!
'Cause a catfish wanna go home! Yeah yeah yeah!
A catfish wanna go home! Yeah yeah yeah!"

"Cut ya?"
"Yeah."
"Cut ya up?"
"Yeah! Yeah! Yeah!"

And so Simon ... he got out a knife, and he did everything that you have to do if you want to eat a fish that you caught. He cut open the stomach, and he took out all of the guts. He cut the skin off of that catfish and when he was done ... he had a beautiful catfish fillet with a head at one end and a tail at the other.

"Si-i-i-i-mon ... Si-i-i-i-mon—"

Simon was so started he nearly dropped his knife. "Yaaah!!!"

"Cook me up, Simon! Cook me up, Simon!
'Cause a catfish wanna go home! Yeah yeah yeah!
A catfish wanna go home! Yeah yeah yeah!"

"Ooohh ... okay ..." said Simon. He got out a pan ... put a little olive oil in it ... a little salt and pepper on the side ... put that catfish fillet in a little bit of flour ... and then he started frying that fish—sssssss—until it was all good and gold on one side ...

Then that catfish FLIPPED itself over in the pan—sssssss—and cooked itself until it was all good and golden on the other side. And you know what?
That catfish rolled a fried eyeball up at Simon and said,

"Si-i-i-i-mon ... Si-i-i-i-mon ...
Eat me up, Simon! Eat me up, Simon!
'Cause a catfish wanna go home! Yeah yeah yeah!
A catfish wanna go home! Yeah yeah yeah!"

"Eat ya?"
"Yeah."
"Eat ya up?"
"Yeah! Yeah! Yeah!"

And so Simon took that fish and put it on a plate.
He got out a knife and fork and began to eat it.
He tried a little bit of the tail. "Mmm. Oh, that was really good!"
He tried a little bit in the middle. "Oh, delicious!"
He tried a little bit of the head. "Oh, it's so good!
MNNNMNNNMMNMMNMNN!"
He ate that whole fish right up! *(Burp!)*
Whew! Simon was so glad to have that talking fish gone
because it was bossing him around so much. And then...

"SI-I-I-MON! SI-I-I-MON!"

"YAAAAHHHH!" Poor Simon was clutching his stomach!

"Take me to the river, Simon! Take me to the river, Simon!
'Cause a catfish wanna go home! Yeah yeah yeah!
A catfish wanna go home! Yeah yeah yeah!"

Simon went running out of his house ...
"AYYYYYY!" ...
down to the side of the river ...
And when he got there that fish said,

"Si-i-i-i-mon ... Si-i-i-i-mon ...
Wade in the water, Simon! Wade in the water, Simon!
'Cause a catfish wanna go home! Yeah yeah yeah!
A catfish wanna go home! Yeah yeah yeah!"

Simon ... he got down to the water ...
And you know what happened next?

That catfish LEAPED right out of his mouth.
Like nothing was the matter with it.
Like it wasn't cooked at all!
It had all its skin ... all its guts inside it ... and it JUMPED
into the water!
And as it was swimming away ... all you could see was a little
tiny fin above the water ... making a tiny wake. And a little
bubbly voice saying ...

"Si-i-i-i-mon ... Si-i-i-i-mon ...
Don't you cut school no more, Simon!
Don't you cut school no more, Simon!
'Cause a catfish wanna go home! Yeah yeah yeah!
A catfish wanna go home! Yeah yeah yeah!"

And that's the story of Si-i-i-mon and the magic catfish.

Story Notes

I learned this story from my mother-in-law, Margaret Read
MacDonald, in October 1997. Driving back from our island cabin,
the car broke down, and while we stood in the weeds by the roadside
waiting for a tow truck, my mother-in-law told us Halloween stories.
I used them the next day in the Tacoma school where I was teaching
and enjoyed this tale so much that it has become my signature story.
Margaret says she created the story from a brief tale in Carl Withers'
book, I Saw a Rocket Walk a Mile (New York: Henry Holt & Co.,
1974). I've adapted the tale and elaborated some of the episodes. In
Margaret's tale Simon skips church. She points out that the tale
appears in British tradition with the church motif and the fish likely

*as the Devil. In the Withers version the boy is never again seen after
his disagreeable fish feast. Stories in which an eaten thing takes over
from inside the stomach appear in several African traditions, Indian
tales, and elsewhere.*

*When I tell the story, I play with the name Simon. Audiences love
it when you stretch the name out and have them repeat it with you—
just like you are a bossy catfish—"Si-i-i-i-mon ... Si-i-i-i-mon ..."*

*I also like to have the audience jump up and dance with me on
the refrain: "'Cause a catfish wanna go home! Yeah yeah yeah! A
catfish wanna go home! Yeah yeah yeah!" You can use it as a rap with
the audience clapping the beat. It is a great chance for everyone to
stretch and have fun.*

NAT WHITMAN has been an international educator since 2001
and currently teaches at the Bonn International School in
Germany. He and his wife, Jennifer, tell in tandem as the
Whitman Story Sampler. They have conducted workshops at
conferences sponsored by the National Storytelling Network,
East Asia Regional Council of Overseas Schools, and the
European Council of International Schools.

The Red Satin Ribbon

An American Variant of a European Legend
Martha Hamilton and Mitch Weiss

Sam and Sue lived next door to each other from the time they were born. Every day they played together. Sam *loved* Sue, and Sue *loved* Sam.

Sam thought Sue was the sweetest, smartest, and most gorgeous girl he'd ever met. She wore such bright, colorful clothes, and every day she wore a red satin ribbon around her neck.

Sue thought that Sam was the nicest, most considerate, and most handsome boy in the world. Sam *loved* Sue, and Sue *loved* Sam.

They went to kindergarten and then first grade together, and every day Sue wore that red ribbon around her neck. Sam began to wonder *why* Sue always wore that ribbon.

One day, he just had to ask, "Susie, why do you always wear that red ribbon around your neck?"

"Oh, I'll tell you later, Sammy," said Sue shyly.

The years passed by, and still Sam *loved* Sue, and Sue *loved* Sam. They went steady all through high school, and every day Sue wore that ribbon around her neck. Sam continued to ask her about it but she'd just say, "I'll tell you later!"

It was the only secret that Sue kept from Sam, but still Sam *loved* Sue, and Sue *loved* Sam.

At last, it was the night of the senior prom. Naturally, Sue and Sam went together. Sue wore a beautiful red satin gown to match the ribbon around her neck.

"Sue, why do you always wear that red ribbon?" Sam begged.

"Why do you always ask me that?" snapped Sue. "It's none of your business! If I feel like it, maybe I'll tell you later."

The years passed by, and, although they argued now and then, still Sam *loved* Sue, and Sue *loved* Sam. Eventually, they became engaged.

On their wedding day, Sam pleaded, "Sue, why do you always wear that red ribbon around your neck? Can't you take it off just this once?"

"Sammy, darling," said Sue, firmly yet lovingly, "I'll take this ribbon off when I'm good and ready. Now please, let's not argue on our wedding day."

The years passed by, and still Sam *loved* Sue, and Sue *loved* Sam. They had two children and several grandchildren. Every day Sue wore that red satin ribbon around her neck. Sam continued to ask her about it, but each time she'd say, "I'll tell you later!"

At last, it was their fiftieth wedding anniversary. Sam was sure that Sue would finally tell him her secret after their many years together.

"Sue, won't you tell me your secret?" said Sam. "Why do you always wear that red satin ribbon around your neck?"

"Sammy, don't you ever get tired of asking me that?" replied Sue. "If I've told you once, I've told you a thousand times. I'll tell you later!"

The years passed by, and still Sam *loved* Sue, and Sue *loved* Sam. But then Sue grew ill, and finally she was on her deathbed. Sam knew they had had a wonderful life together, but still he was heartbroken. And there was one thing he had to know before she died.

Kneeling by her bed, tears streaming down his cheeks, he pleaded with her one last time. "Susie, we've known each other for more than eighty years, and every day you've worn that red ribbon tied around your neck. Won't you please tell me why you wear it?"

"Well, Sam, you've been so patient all these years," said Sue, her voice shaking. "If you must know, I'll show you."

With her last bit of strength, Sue took hold of one end of the red satin ribbon and began to untie it,

and as she did ...

    her

        head

            fell

                off.

Story Notes

We have told this story for twenty-nine years and still enjoy it, especially the surprise ending. This tale is unusual in that it can be told for Valentine's Day and Halloween! If you enjoy doing character voices, do little-kid voices for young Sam and Sue, older voices for them when it's their fiftieth wedding anniversary, and somewhat shaky voices when Sue is on her deathbed. Use body language and expression in your voice to show that, as time passes, Sam gets more and more curious about why Sue wears the ribbon. At the same time, show that Sue grows more frustrated with his frequent questions.

As you say the last sentence, it's important to go very slowly to keep listeners in suspense about why Sue has always worn the red ribbon. When you say "her head fell off," use lots of expression— amazement or confusion or disgust, or perhaps a combination of all these feelings. Before we begin our story, we tell listeners that if they know the ending, they can join in and say the last four words with us, but that they shouldn't tell anyone before that.

We found versions of this story in The Rainbow Book of American Folktales and Legends *by Maria Leach (Cleveland: World, 1958) and in* In a Dark, Dark Room and Other Scary Stories *by Alvin Schwartz (New York: HarperTrophy, 1985). Folklorist Leach noted that this folktale is the offspring of an old*

European folk motif where a person has a strange red thread around his neck that turns out to be the mark that was caused when he was decapitated. Washington Irving's "The Adventures of the German Student" in his Tales of a Traveler *included this motif.*

MARTHA HAMILTON AND MITCH WEISS are known as "Beauty and the Beast Storytellers." A team since 1980, this husband and wife have traveled as far as Japan and Hong Kong to tell their tales. Their previous books and recordings include *How and Why Stories, Noodlehead Stories, Through the Grapevine, Scared Witless, The Hidden Feast* (illustrated by Don Tate), *The Ghost Catcher* (illustrated by Kristen Balouch), and *Priceless Gifts* (illustrated by John Kanzler). They live in Ithaca, New York.

The Dauntless Girl

A British Folktale
Margaret Read MacDonald

There was a girl named Mary who worked for a farmer.
One night that farmer was sitting up with some friends, playing cards,
and they got to talking about their hired girls.
They started to brag about what great servants they had.
"I've got the best hired girl in the county," said one.
"She can cook and clean ... keeps everything *spotless*."
"My hired girl is even better," said another.
"She can cook and clean *and* she feeds the chickens, hoes the
garden, and milks the cow."

Now the farmer spoke up.
"*You* may have great servants, but *my* hired girl beats all of yours.
This girl, Mary, is completely dauntless.
She is not afraid of ANYTHING.
She never calls me to come kill a snake, or a spider ...
She just takes care of it herself.
If she is down in the cellar getting a jar of fruit up
and a mouse runs across her feet ... she never squeals.
She just says, 'Hmm ... time to set a mousetrap.'
If she is up in the attic looking for something
and a spider runs across her nose ... she never yelps.
She just says, 'Hmm ... better clean up those spiderwebs.'
If she is walking down the road past the cemetery

late at night and hears something down in there going
'Oooooooohhhhhhh' ... she won't holler and run.
She just says, 'Hmm ... wonder what's the matter with *that* old ghost?'
She is totally DAUNTLESS!"

His friends looked at one another.
They didn't quite believe him.
Now one of these friends happened to be a doctor, and he had
an idea.
The doctor said, "I will bet one hundred dollars that I can find
something that will scare the wits out of your Mary."
"I'll bet a hundred dollars on my Mary," said the farmer.
"NOTHING will scare *that* girl."
So they shook hands on the bet.

"Be back here at eleven o'clock tomorrow night," said the doctor.
"And we will *see* how dauntless Mary is."

Now this doctor knew the man who took care of the cemetery.
He went to talk to this fellow.
The doctor said, "I'll give you fifty dollars if you'll hide in the
mausoleum tonight at midnight.
I'm going to send a girl down there by the name of Mary.
I want you to scare the wits out of her."

Well, the cemetery keeper wasn't too eager to hang around the
cemetery after dark.
He didn't mind tending the graves during the daytime.
Nighttime was a different matter.
But for fifty dollars? He said, "I'll do it."

So that night, just before midnight, he hid himself behind the
mausoleum door.

He left the door open a crack, because he was scared to be shut
in there in the dark with all those dead folks.
Then he waited.

The farmer and his card-playing friends met at eleven o'clock
just as planned.
"Bring down your hired girl, Mary," said the doctor.
"Let's *see* how dauntless she is."

So Mary was called in.
"I've got a job for you tonight, Mary," said the doctor.
"I want you to go down to the cemetery ...
and go into the mausoleum ...
and bring me back a skull bone."
"What do you want a *skull* bone for?" asked Mary.
"Never you mind. Will you *do* it?"
"If that's what you want," said Mary.
And she put on her shawl and went off down the road.

It was just midnight when she reached the cemetery.
The mausoleum door was open a crack.
"Well, that's luck," said Mary. "It's unlocked."
She pushed the door open wide.
There was no light inside, but the moonlight shone in the door
enough for her to see shelves from floor to ceiling
all around that room.
And on every shelf ... piles of dead people's bones.
Mary walked right in and looked around.
Picked up a bone ... "No, that's a shin bone."
Picked up another ... "No, that's an arm bone."
Picked up another ... "Looks like a shoulder bone."
Bent over and picked up another ... "THERE'S a head bone."

She put the bone under her arm and started out the door.
But just then that old fellow hiding behind the door started in.
"Ooooooo …
Put that baaaaack …
That's my FATHER'S skull!"

"Oh. Sorry about that," said Mary.
And she put the skull bone back.
Looked around and picked up another one.
Tucked it under her arm and started to leave.

"Ooooooo …
Put that baaaaack …
That's my MOTHER'S skull!"

"Beg your pardon," said Mary.
She put that one back and looked around to find another.
Tucked it under her arm.

"Ooooooo …
Put that baaaaack …
That's my BROTHER'S skull!"

"Good grief! They're all *related*!"
She put it back and picked out another.
Tucked it under her arm and turned …

"Ooooooo …
Put that baaaaack …
That's my SISTER'S skull!"

"Well mother or father, sister or brother,
I've got to have a SKULL BONE!" said Mary.

And she stuffed it under her arm, walked out, and closed the door.
As soon as she closed that door, the old 'ghost' inside started
hollering.
"WHOOP! WHOOP!
Let me OUT!
WHOOP! WHOOP!
Open the DOOR!
WHOOP! WHOOP!
It's DARK in here!
WHOOP! WHOOP!
Open the DOOR!"

"Laws!" said Mary. "That ghost is wanting to get OUT."
And she turned around and locked that door up tight.
"Don't want *ghosts* roaming around the country.
THAT will keep him in."
And she walked off down the road.
She could hear that old ghost just a-whooping inside that
mausoleum.

"WHOOP! WHOOP!
Let me OUT!
WHOOP! WHOOP!
Open this DOOR!"

Mary walked right into that farmer's kitchen
and plopped that skull bone down on the table.
"Yuck! A human skull bone!"
Those men all jumped back.
"You really did it, Mary?" The men were amazed.
"Weren't you scared?" they gasped.
"What on earth was there to be scared of?" said Mary.
"They were all DEAD. And I was ALIVE."

"Didn't you hear anything there?" asked the doctor.
"Oh yes," said Mary.
"There was a grumpy old ghost behind the door.
He kept hollering about his mother and his father
and his sister and his brother.
But I told him I *had* to have a skull bone.
So I just took one and left.
He wanted to get out when I left. But I locked that door up tight.
You don't have to worry about *him* roaming the country.
You should have heard him hollering."

When the doctor heard that, he knew that his friend must be locked inside that mausoleum.
He jumped up and ran back down the road to the cemetery.
There wasn't a sound coming from the mausoleum now.
When he unlocked the door and looked inside, he saw a horrible sight.
His friend was lying stone dead on the cold floor.
That poor man had died of *fright* from being locked in with all those dead bones.
And his hair had turned pure white from the terror.

But that girl Mary ... she had proved dauntless indeed.
So they gave her the whole hundred dollars.
And they all admitted ... that Mary *was* a DAUNTLESS GIRL.

$tory Notes

Retold from A Dictionary of British Folk-Tales *by Katharine M. Briggs (Bloomington: Indiana University Press, 1970), pp. 204–206. Briggs took her tale from W. Rye,* The Recreations of a Norfolk Antiquary *(New York: Henry Holt, 1920), which she believes came from an oral source, and from the F.J. Norton Collection, ms. vol. 1, pp. 152–154. Motifs are H1400 Fear test and H1435 Fetching skulls from a charnelhouse.*

MARGARET READ MACDONALD has written more than fifty books on folklore and storytelling topics. If you like this book, you might also like her *When the Lights Go Out: Twenty Scary Stories to Tell* and *Ghost Stories from the Pacific Northwest*—or you may enjoy the magical tales in *The Singing Top: Tales from Malaysia, Singapore, and Brunei.* If you want to learn how to tell stories like this see *The Storyteller's Start-up Book.* MacDonald lives in Seattle but travels the world sharing tales and discovering new ones. Find out more at www.margaretreadmacdonald.com.

Shut Up, Billy!

An Original Tale with a Traditional Twist
Jim May

Summer nights four of us would go camping next to the woods behind my parents' house. Gary, Billy, and I were all in fifth grade; Butch was in eighth. He was bigger and stronger. His voice was getting lower and he was starting to get a mustache. The rest of us were a little afraid of Butch, but he was a pretty good guy and could really hit a baseball; we lived in a small town, and we needed everyone we could find to make up a team.

Butch liked to camp, except for one thing. He didn't like ghost stories. Billy loved to tell them. Actually, Billy was the only one of us who liked ghost stories. We would just be falling asleep in our tent, wondering about the night sounds we were hearing—tree limbs rubbing together, animals scurrying in the underbrush—and Billy would start in: "Hey, you guys, did you hear about the werewolf of Fish Hatchery Road?"

"No," I'd say.

Gary would laugh nervously.

"Shut up, Billy," Butch would say.

That was usually the end of it … for a while.

One summer night after supper, the four of us headed out to camp. It took three of us to drag the heavy green canvas wall tent along the ground. It must have weighed a thousand pounds. Gary, Billy, and I took turns pulling it along the ground and carrying the tent poles.

"Hey, Butch. How about helping out?" asked Gary, grunting and straining as he pulled the bulky tent through the weeds.

"I got my own bag I'm carrying," said Butch.

"Jeez," Gary muttered to himself. Butch had a pillowcase with a candy bar and a bag of marshmallows. He wasn't even carrying his own sleeping bag; he had made Gary stuff it into his backpack.

"Yeah, Butch," said Billy. "Why don't you help with the tent for a while?"

"Don't want to," said Butch.

"You think we're just dying to drag this thing?" Billy said.

Butch said nothing. He wasn't a big talker.

We stopped in an open field right next to the woods. The woods were thick with oak and hickory trees. On the other side of the woods was a swamp with dense willow thickets and a meandering creek. If the wind was right you could smell the mud and the rot. The swamp made us uneasy that night because earlier in the summer we had seen a movie, *The Creature from the Black Swamp*, about a scary reptilian-like thing that had emerged from a swamp and terrorized a small town.

Billy had seen the movie and told us all about it. "You guys, it was cool! The creature had jaws like a giant snapping turtle. It grabbed little kids by the legs when they were walking by the swamp and pulled them under and drowned them, just the way turtles drown baby ducks. Then it would flop the kid's limp body back up onto the bank and chew and slobber all over it, but what it loved most was the eyeballs! It had this long tongue with barbed spikes, and it would snarl and slobber and spear the kid's eyeballs with its tongue and then take the rest of the body down to the bottom of the pond and chew on it for weeks until it was all putrid and decayed. Eventually some parts—pieces of ears and noses and clumps of hair—would float up to the top, and THAT WAS ALL THAT WOULD BE LEFT OF THE KID!"

We called off camping for a couple of weeks, thanks to Billy.

No one mentioned the movie that night, but we all were in a hurry to get our tent up before dark and build a fire for protection.

It wasn't long before darkness shrouded everything and the fire had burned down. Our faces shone red in the glow of the coals. The moon drifted in and out of the clouds as we lay around the fire. The coals hissed. The smell of smoke hung in the air, and stars filled the black sky. We weren't the toughest kids or the coolest guys or the best baseball players; but the stars belonged to us for that little while next to the red coal fire.

"You think there's a werewolf on Fish Hatchery Road?" Gary asked.

"Nah," I said.

"Maybe." Billy smiled. "That's what Wayne Moore says. He was at Carl Bartolini's house, and the Ouija board told him he would see a werewolf by the bridge and so he was afraid to ride his bike home. So he called his dad to get him in the car. His dad put the bike in the trunk and drive him home. Wayne said he saw a hairy thing crouched in the ditch by the bridge, next to the culvert, ready to spring. He said his dad saw something, too, and floored the gas pedal, and they peeled out of there."

We scooted a little closer to the fire. It was well known that a fire would repel all kinds of werewolves—and wild swamp monsters, too.

"Hey Gary, you know that long driveway by the haunted house by the lumber yard?" asked Billy.

"Yeah."

"I dare you to walk down there trick-or-treating next Halloween."

"Yeah, I'll do it," said Gary. "I don't believe what they say about that girl dying in there and her parents leaving the body in the basement and moving away."

"Oh right," Billy said sarcastically. "You were afraid to go to the monkey house last Halloween."

"Oh, yeah? First of all, that wasn't a monkey, it was a gorilla. My uncle saw him looking out the window," countered Gary.

"That place has been empty since before your uncle was born, and it wasn't a gorilla, it was a monkey, a little spider monkey," insisted Billy.

"Well, ah … maybe it was the *ghost* of some gorilla," Gary said defensively.

"Kind of creepy, huh?" said Billy. "So much weird stuff going on in such a small town?"

"Last one in the tent is dead!" I yelled, jumping toward the front tent flap. In the movies, the last one left outside the tent alone always gets picked off by whatever is out there. I was in the lead. No werewolf was going to get me!

I hit the canvas on the run, crumpled, and fell. Then the rest of them ran into me and fell into a pile. The tent was zippered shut. We plastered up against the mosquito-proof screen door like bugs on a windshield.

"You dope, why didn't you unzip the door?" asked Gary.

"Hey, I just got here." I said.

Everyone backed off. I fumbled around with the zipper.

"Hurry up. I hear something out there," said Billy, laughing.

"Do not!" sneered Butch.

"Do, too!"

"Hurry up," Gary yelled.

Finally, I got the tent open and we tumbled inside. We climbed into our sleeping bags and got real quiet.

We could still sense the movement of the moon and clouds by the play of light and shadow through the cracks in the tent canvas.

"Nothing out there," said Butch, "but raccoons and owls."

"Yeah, just regular animals," said Gary.

"You wish," chuckled Billy, who now had his flashlight under his chin. "I'm the wwweeeerrrrewooolf of Fish Hatchery Road."

"OK, knock it off!" said Butch. "I want it quiet! Quiet! I wanna sleep."

We got quiet. All you could hear were tree frogs and crickets and maybe something else … but we tried not to listen. I was already wishing for the morning, when it would be sunny and warm and everything would look familiar again. The sun would burn off all the hidden, creepy things, sending all the inky creatures scurrying back to their shadowy havens, leaving us the summer day—if we could just fall asleep.

"What was that?" asked Billy.

"What?" I answered.

"I heard something," he whispered.

"Did not," said Butch

"Yeah, I did. There!" insisted Billy.

We all heard it now. It was a scream, like a woman or a child—insistent, rising and falling—then something scrambling in the leaves close to the tent.

"Yikes," Billy laughed.

"Just a raccoon," Gary said.

"No, I don't think so, maybe a rabbit," I said. "Nothing screams like a dying rabbit. Maybe a fox got it." I knew that fox hunters used calls like that to call in foxes.

It got quiet again, but now we weren't even close to sleeping.

That's when Billy started in with another story. He always picked the worst times.

"Did you guys ever hear about Bloody Mary? You know, you go into your bathroom and turn the lights off, and, and you say three times: 'Bloody Mary, Bloody Mary, Bloody Mary …' and you look in the mirror and … want to hear it?"

"No," I said.

Gary laughed nervously.

"Shut up, Billy!" said Butch.

We got real quiet again. More tree frogs and then …
something moving, heavy footsteps near our tent.

"What's that?" Gary asked.

"I don't know!" I said weakly.

Then we heard a loud, desperate neighing, real close.

"It's just one of my dad's horses over in the pasture," I said.
I hoped I was right.

"Horses?" said Billy. "Did you ever hear about the zombie
horses of Volo Bog?"

"Oh no, now what?" Gary said. We all groaned.

"Yeah, yeah," said Billy. "Zombie horses with big crazed
smiles. Well, they don't exactly smile, but it looks like it because
their lips have shrunk away after they've been dead and you just
see these big white teeth, and their hooves are like a blue mass
of jelly and pus, and their eyes are yellow like the cold moon, and
they live at Volo Bog over by Fox Lake. It's a creepy place. The
water is the color of dried blood, and the plants that grow there
can digest meat! There's practically no bottom to the bog. You
can be walking along on spongy ground and then just fall right
through and get sucked down."

"Yeah, I heard of that," I said. "In science class Sister Cristella
said that bog water has no oxygen and so much acid that someone
could get sucked down into it and never decompose. They found
a three-thousand-year-old body in a bog in Denmark."

"That's right," said Billy. "Those zombie horses are still
there, because that's where they died, and some zombie farmer is
there, too. They say a long time ago his horses got out, and he
went to look for them under a full moon with the wind blowing,
like … like tonight. The horses were neighing because they were
scared of being lost, but the sound of their calls got to blowing
around in the wind, and the farmer got confused and lost his
direction, and the horses did, too. They all disappeared—just got
sucked down into the bog. Never heard from. As the farmer was

drowning he looked up through the amber water at the full moon. If you die under a full moon, you become among the undead and you can't rest when the moon is full. I heard that the farmer is still in the bog now with those horses and their glowing eyes and their teeth and they could follow the creek all the way from the bog and they could be HERE! You want to hear more?"

"No!" I said.

Gary laughed nervously

"SHUT UP, BILLY!" said Butch. He began climbing out of his sleeping bag, his hand in a fist, shaking it at Billy.

Billy dove into his sleeping bag and zipped it up.

Quiet again. We listened to more noises outside— scampering, low whistles, and maybe a screaming rabbit.

Billy broke the silence. "There was this fourth grader—"

"SHUT UP, BILLY!" We all yelled it this time.

"No, wait! This isn't scary, honest," Billy argued. "He lived on the fourth floor of an apartment building. He had never stayed at home alone before. One day his mother said, 'I'm going to the store. I'll only be gone one hour. Just behave and I'll be back in a little while.'

"The boy watched his mother go out the door. He stood in the doorway watching her walk down the hallway to the elevator. He closed the door and ran to the window. He watched his mother come out of the lobby onto the street below. She looked at him and waved. He watched her go down the sidewalk and turn the corner. She was gone!

"He ran back into the kitchen and began opening drawers. Found the candy bars! 'Yes!' Found the doughnuts! 'Yes!' He went to the cupboard and started pulling out small bottles and shaker jars: vanilla, cinnamon, cloves, jalapeño powder, black pepper, cayenne, vinegar, baking soda. He was planning a chemistry experiment!

"And then the phone rang.

"The boy picked up the phone: 'Hello?'"

"*I am the viper. I am on the first floor.*"

Billy drew in his breath. No one said anything.

"The boy hung up the phone," Billy continued. "'What's this? A joke? I wonder when Mom's coming back?'

"He looked at the clock over the refrigerator. She'd been gone fifteen minutes.

"He returned to mixing up his new scientific breakthrough. The phone rang again! Slowly he walked over to the phone."

Billy reached out like he was picking the phone up, his hand shaking a little.

"'Hello …?'

"*I am the viper. I am on the second floor.*'

"The boy slammed the phone down. 'Where's Mom?'"

We all laughed.

"The boy looked again at the clock on the wall. His mom had been gone half an hour. He began to pace back and forth.

"The phone rang again. The boy froze in his tracks. It rang again, and again, and again."

"DON'T PICK UP THE PHONE!" screamed Gary. "Call the police!"

We all laughed at Gary. Butch punched him in the arm.

"Finally the boy grabbed the phone." Billy's hand was shaking violently and his voice was high-pitched and shrill. "'There's nobody home,' the boy whispered.

"*I am the viper. I am on the third floor.*'

"The boy slammed down the phone, whimpering."

More laughter. Even Butch laughed.

"The boy dove for the couch and pulled a blanket over himself." Billy dove under his sleeping bag in mock horror. We all laughed some more. "He couldn't move; he lay under a quilt on the couch.

"Then … there came a slow, heavy pounding on the door.

"The boy didn't really want to know who was at the door, but he didn't want to be trapped in the room, either. He had to face the music. He grabbed a wooden chair in one hand, a baseball bat in the other, and he slowly opened the door.

"There, filling up the entire doorway, was a huge man. He was carrying a long pole in one hand, a steel bucket in the other. At the end of the pole was a mop.

"'I am the viper,' he said. 'I come to vipe your vindows.'"

We all groaned. We all looked at Billy. And together we yelled: "Shut up, Billy!"

Story Notes

I often begin a program of ghost stories by recalling how much fun it is to tell ghost stories to friends around a campfire or at stay-over parties. The opening scenes of this story recall those memories. I then tell a traditional or original ghost story after setting up the listeners with their own memories of their anticipation of retelling the story they are about to hear to their friends.

"The Viper" is a traditional story, passed down by young people, from one to another, orally, through the generations. It's a "playground ghost story" that I've heard over the years—not only as a child myself but as an elementary school teacher and as a storyteller. This is my current version of that basic story.

I encourage my young readers to take these stories and personalize them, make them your own. You might have to tell it just as it reads for awhile until you get your own ideas, but then don't be afraid to make the story your own original adaptation.

JIM MAY is an Emmy award-winning storyteller and author. His book, *The Farm on Nippersink Creek: Stories from a Midwestern Childhood*, was named a Best New Book for Young Readers by the Public Library Association. His picture book, *The Boo Baby Girl Meets the Ghost of Mable's Gable*, is a favorite of teachers and librarians. When Jim isn't conducting author visits or writing/storytelling workshops, he lives with his wife, Nancy Seidler, a visual artist, in Alden, Illinois. Their farm is on the headwaters of the Nippersink Creek, where they garden, restore native habitat, and ride horses with their granddaughters, Katrina and Izabelle.

Urban Legends
and Jump Tales

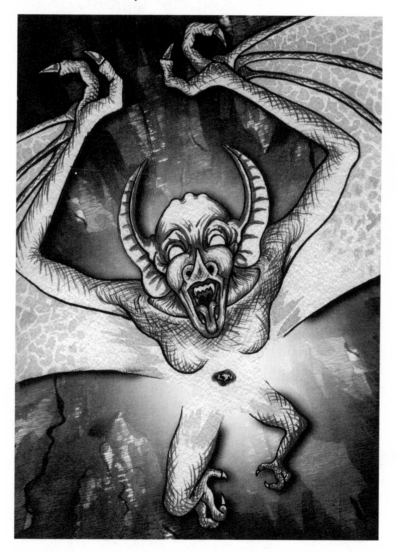

Ain't Nobody Here

An African-American Folktale
Lyn Ford

An old man sat in front of the fireplace one evening, just sat and rocked, warming his feet by the fire. The fire crackled. The rocking chair creaked. Then a thing slowly rose in the flames, stepped out of the fire, and stood in front of the man.

They just looked at one another, that thing and that man.

Without saying a word, that thing sat down in the second rocking chair and started rocking right in time with that man— *cccrrreak, cccrrrreak, cccrrreak* ...

They rocked that way a long, long time. The fire crackled. The rocking chairs creaked.

Then that thing turned to the man and grinned and said, "Man, ain't nobody sittin' here rockin' by the fire, nobody rockin' but you and me."

Well, that man jumped right out of that rocking chair, ran right through the front door without opening it, lurched down the porch stairs, and raced down the road. That old man ran faster than any old man had ever run.

As his bare feet slapped against the road, that old man heard something close behind him. He felt something warm on the back of his neck. He looked over his shoulder.

There was that thing, breathing its foul breath on him, and running just as fast as he was.

That thing grinned and said, "Man, ain't nobody runnin' down this here road, nobody runnin' but you and me."

That man ran faster than any man, old or young, had ever run. His heart nearly pounded its way out of his chest; his lungs burned as he struggled to get away from that thing.

A wall of smooth stone stood at the bend in the road. The old man fell against that wall, then leaned against it and panted as he tried to catch his breath. He looked down the road to see if that thing was near.

It was. That thing was leaning against the wall, right beside the man, close enough to tickle that old man's neck with its long dirty fingernails.

That thing grinned and said, "Man, ain't nobody leanin' up against this here wall, nobody leanin' but you and me."

That old man started to climb that wall, but the stones were smooth. The old man slid and slipped and slid some more. And right next to him was that thing, climbing and slipping and sliding and grinning, as it said, "Man, ain't nobody tryin' to climb this here wall, nobody climbin' but you and me."

The old man quickly reached the top of the wall—a little too quickly, for he lost his grip. He slipped and fell—*THUMP!*—on the other side of the wall.

That thing reached the top of the wall and jumped— *THUMP!*—and landed on the old man. It pushed itself up and looked that old man in the eye. It grinned and said, "Man, ain't nobody here on the ground, nobody here but you and me."

That's when the old man passed out.

The next morning, somebody came along and saw that old man beside the wall. That somebody shook the old man until he revived and helped him up from the ground. That somebody dusted off the old man's clothes and put an arm around his shoulder.

"Poor man!" said that somebody. "Please, tell me, what happened to you?"

The old man trembled and nearly cried. "L-last night," he said, "a th-th-thing stepped out of my fireplace. It chased me out of my house, down this road, and up this wall. Then it jumped on me. And I ... I guess I passed out."

"Oh," said that somebody, "how terrible! But don't worry now, man. You see, there's nobody here, nobody here ... but *you* ... and ... ME!"

Story Notes

This is my adaptation of an African-American ghost-race tale; my version is based on the story as told by my father, Edward M. Cooper. There are many versions of this story, which can be traced to similar tales in Africa. One was noted by Maria Leach in her book, Whistle in the Graveyard: Folktales to Chill Your Bones *(New York: Puffin Books, 1982. First published by The Viking Press, 1974. See p. 28, "Nobody Here But You and Me"). For similar stories, see "Never Mind Them Watermelons," a ghost-race tale retold by S. E. Schlosser, at her website, http://www.americanfolklore.net/folktales/al2.html, and "Talk," a story of incredible talking things that frighten people into running away, in* The Cow-tail Switch and Other West African Stories *by Harold Courlander and George Herzog (reissued; New York: Feiwel and Friends, 2008). The motif for "Nobody Here" is Host converses with man running from him, J1495.1.*

This is a really fun story to tell. Each time I say the phrase "but you and me," I point to one of my listeners. At the end of the story, when the phrase is repeated for the last time, I let my pointing finger sweep the entire audience. I give "the thing" a raspy, whispering voice that comes from a slyly grinning face. When "the thing" falls on the man, I loudly clap one hand on the other for a slightly startling effect. The final words begin in a normal, friendly manner, accompanied by gestures of caring and concern, then slowly become the raspy, whispering statement of "the thing."

LYN FORD's love of strange and spooky stories began in childhood. Her father told "spookers and haints" tales that made her laugh … but kept her awake. As a fourth-generation storyteller and a teaching artist, Lyn has traveled the country sharing folktale adaptations and original stories rooted in her family's multicultural "Afrilachian" oral traditions. She lives in Reynoldsburg, Ohio.

Outside the Door

Based on U.S. Campus Lore
Richard and Judy Dockrey Young

It was the holidays, and most of the kids had gone home from boarding school for a week. Some of the students, however, lived too far away, or their parents were out of the country, or someone was coming to pick them up later in the week. To save electricity and heating oil, all the students from all the dorms were moved into two dorms temporarily, one for guys and one for gals.

In the girls' dorm, two girls who had never met were put in a room together. They hit it off well from the first, and the sun had long set when they got back from the dining commons that night and went to their room.

The older girl told the younger girl that she had seen someone in the shadows outside the dorm, and they agreed to keep the door to the room locked. Then the older girl went down the hall to take a shower.

She was gone a long time, and the younger girl began to get scared. She stood with her ear against the locked door of the room, hoping to hear the older girl coming down the hall. What she heard terrified her.

It was a noise like a huge snake, sliding down the hall and moving slowly toward the door. Then she heard a gurgling sound, like a monster blowing bubbles in the water of a lagoon. Then something began to claw at the door, scratching as if it wanted to get in.

The younger girl screamed.

What *was* that thing outside the room—some kind of huge, hideous animal that crawled like a snake and clawed at the door? The scratching went on and on! Was it some kind of maniac? What weapon did he have? Was he cutting slowly through the door?

The younger girl retreated from the door into a corner away from the windows. She slid slowly down into a seated position and began to cry. The scratching, clawing sound went on.

For hours.

The girl cried herself to sleep.

When she woke up, it was bright outside, long after sunrise. There was no sound at all in the dorm. There was no sound at all in the hall. The younger girl walked slowly to the door.

Did she dare to open it?

She gently took hold of the knob with one hand.

Was the monster waiting just outside, waiting for her to open the door?

She took the knob of the door lock in the other hand.

Was the maniac just down the hall with his weapon, waiting?

Slowly she turned the lock.

Slowly she turned the knob.

Slowly she opened the door.

On the hall floor was the other girl, dead in a pool of blood. Her throat had been cut. The door was covered with scratches from her fingernails. She had been trying to get the younger girl to let her in.

Story Notes

Richard first heard this story in the early 1960s at the University of Arkansas in Fayetteville, when Bill Clinton was on faculty at the university law school and was Richard's next-door neighbor. The story was told to incoming freshmen in a time when holiday stays in dorms were a common practice. When telling this story, the teller should first act reluctant to share it, saying something evasive like "I promised never to talk about this again." During the story, the teller should look from side to side as if to see if somehow the wrong people are listening. Tell it softly, getting quieter and quieter as if you are sharing a terrible secret. This is not a jump story; it should end with the teller relaying a sense of grief and the listeners feeling their flesh crawl.

RICHARD AND JUDY DOCKREY YOUNG are professional storytellers who have performed at Silver Dollar City, an historic theme park in Branson, Missouri, for more than thirty years. Their specialty has always been Ozark myths and legends. They have co-authored nine folktale collections with August House since 1989. They reside at the edge of the Mark Twain National Forest in the wilds of Stone County, Missouri. In the winter off-season, they perform at schools, libraries, and festivals. They maintain a website at www.yawp.com/stories.

Tío Mono y La Lechusa

Based on Mexican Folk Legend
Gregorio C. Pedroza

Tío Mono is next to the youngest in my mother's family of twenty-four brothers and sisters. He is a gregarious, fun-loving, joking type of a guy. He is only nine years older than me, and as a little boy not yet ten I wanted to be cool like Tío Mono.

Tío Mono had two passions—baseball and dancing. On the baseball field there was no wasted motion. As he shagged a grounder he seemed to float toward the ball; from his dancing feet to his guiding hands he was all fluid motion as he fielded and threw the ball. Even on the baseball field, he danced.

On the dance floor he was so cool it seemed as if the musicians were watching him in order to keep the right tempo. His moves were smooth, and he and his partner seemed to glide as if they were dancing a few inches above the concrete dance floor. His arms guided and led in flowing motions, and his feet moved as if they had a mind of their own. At that time I was a contest-winning dancer myself, but still I had a lot to learn from Tío Mono.

If his girl wanted to stay after the dance to talk he would get home late. If the team wanted to celebrate after an evening game he would get home even later. Or as he would say, "I was home early ... this morning."

Being home late posed no major problem except for Abuelita, who would stay up until everyone was home. Well, perhaps it was also a problem for Tío Mono, for most of the time

he had to walk home alone. We lived in El Barrio de la Rana—
"the neighborhood of the frog." Our *barrio* lacked a few minor
things. Paved streets, streetlights, and sidewalks were dreams for
the future. It was called "the neighborhood of the frog" because
when it rained we would flood and afterwards it seemed that
millions of frogs would emerge in the standing water. So walking
through the *barrio* at night was no walk in the park!

There were a few reference points that helped on dark
moonless nights. Just outside the *barrio* a man had a large
number of guinea hens. They made a ruckus no matter what
time of the day or night anyone came near their coop. So
sneaking back into the *barrio* meant staying quietly in the middle
of the road lest the feathery alarm system alert the whole town.
For guidance there were also the goats whose bells clattered
loudly and Don Pedro's mule and donkey, who snorted when
they sensed you near their corral.

Another sure sign that you were near home was when your
shoes got wet. A wide ditch crossed a low place in the road just
before Abuelita's house. Wet feet made you miserable for a
moment, but it also meant you would be in your warm bed soon.

As soon as Tío Mono would enter the house he would start
talking to whomever was still up. He had a distinct way of
talking. He talked with his whole body and *never* in a low
voice—he would grow so agitated that those who didn't know
him well might think he was angry. In reality he was just excited;
words would trip out of his mouth like many clowns from a small
car. And to top it all off, he stuttered.

One dark night Tío Mono came home extra excited. Once
again, he had stayed out late with the team and walked home—
no, he had *run* home—and he was as white as an uncooked
tortilla. Now there were only two *cucuis*—bogeymen—that we
knew of. One was La Llorona, the wailing woman, but she only
appeared by the water's edge, and the ditch was just muddy this

time of the year. So that couldn't have been it. The other *cucui* was La Lechusa!

Sure enough, as soon as his big boiled-egg-sized eyes could focus and his shaking body could sit in a chair without bouncing off, Tío Mono told us what he had seen.

At first he said he had not been drinking. Then he admitted that he had had a drink but was not drunk. The celebration at a local *cantina* had gone on just a little bit longer than he wanted. No one else wanted to leave so he decided to walk home alone.

Tío Mono smiled as he recounted how once again he had outsmarted those noisy guinea hens. His next reference point after the chicken coop would have been the donkey corral, but he never heard a snort. Instead he heard a cackle.

Now even those of you who grew up in the city know that donkeys don't cackle. And mules and goats don't cackle either. Tío Mono's swagger turned into rapid stutter-steps as he kept looking back over his shoulder. He tried to whistle but all that came out was air. Then he heard the cackle again—this time followed by a blood-curdling screech. Once again he looked back ... and then up ... and then he saw it.

At this point in the story, Tío Mono had to stand up and look out the window before he continued. Abuelita gave him a glass of water and pulled out her rosary just in case it was needed to ward off evil spirits. After he steadied himself, Tío Mono resumed his story.

When he looked back ... and then up ... Tío Mono saw a huge black bird. It had wings like those of a bat and the body of a woman ... or was it a huge woman with the wings of a bat? At any rate, the woman's face was grotesque. She had huge fangs, and gooey stuff dripped from the end of her swollen tongue. Her hair was disheveled, and she had large talons for fingernails.

Tío Mono now knew it was La Lechusa because she carried a light in her belly—not a lantern but a light like a burning ember, a glowing lump of coal that flitted in the night as she dove and swooped and screeched above his head. As La Lechusa passed near trees their limbs would crack, falling before the mighty swings of her arms. The goats and donkey and mule—even the guinea hens—were quiet. No creature in her path wanted to attract her attention!

Tío Mono's feet were moving as though he were trying to steal home, and indeed that is what he was trying to do. He crossed the ditch without getting his shoes wet or even muddy. He flew home on feet of air as La Lechusa screeched and cackled, swooped and dove. He jumped fences even though he could not see them; he just knew they were there. He bumped into trees like a pinball, but he kept running. The light in La Lechusa's belly kept blinking as if it were trying to zero in on him.

Tío Mono was flat-out, bug-eyed, snot-snorting scared. He did not know whether to head for the outhouse or the kitchen first. La Lechusa swooped down, hitting him on the shoulder just as he dove onto the back porch. He did not even remember opening the screen door. He was in the kitchen, breathing in gasps, shaking like a jumping bean in the sun, checking to see if he had wet his pants, and trying to talk all at the same time. At first all he could say was "La Lechusa! La Lechusa!"

Abuelita, in her most serious voice, said, "Son, now you know what awaits those who come home late at night after a night of drinking. La Lechusa will get you unless you mend your ways."

Never again—well, maybe not for a very long while—did Tío Mono come home late. He even suggested that the baseball games be played in the afternoon and that someone walk home with him after the dances. La Lechusa had done her job well.

Story Notes

In our Mexican tradition, death is viewed as a friend, not a scary topic. Besides El Diablo, three major characters are used to keep both children and adults from going out at night or playing in dangerous areas: La Llorona (the "wailing woman"), El Cucui, the general bogeyman, and La Lechusa, who you've just met. Recently El Chupacabras (the "goat sucker") has been added to the lore.

La Lechusa is huge with leathery wings. She shrieks, swoops, and flaps her wings at her prey. Her belly button is a bright red searching light that does not illuminate a path but reveals her intended victim. La Lechusa comes out only at night and attacks mainly boys and men who are out late where they should not be.

This story is written in the caso (event/experience) style, a classic genre of Mexican literature. It can also work as a jump tale, best told in a dimly lit space. The shrieks are accentuated and prolonged. The victim's imagination scares him more than the actual sight of La Lechusa.

GREGORIO C. PEDROZA was born in a Mexican-American barrio in south Texas. In 1967 he attained a Ph.D. in organic chemistry. After a twenty-five-year career as a scientist and manager with IBM, he took a medical retirement and became a bilingual storyteller. Gregorio has entertained audiences of all ages with his original stories in Europe, the Caribbean, Central and South America, and throughout the U.S. His scholarship foundation, Firekeeper Fund, Inc., is registered with the New York State Department of Education. He lives with his wife, Lilly, in Apalachin, New York. Please visit him at www.gpedroza.com.

Johnny and the Dead Man's Liver

An African-American Folktale
James "Sparky" Rucker

Once there was a boy named Johnny, who was a precocious young man and who, sometimes, disobeyed his parents. If they asked him to do a chore he'd often find an excuse—if not every reason in the book—to delay it or disobey it.

One day his mother was planning their dinner, and she decided to have liver and onions. Johnny, who usually *loved* her liver and onions, was asked to go to the butcher shop, which was located in the supermarket, to purchase the liver. Johnny asked his mother, "Mom ... can I also get some candy?" His mother, in the typical mother response, said, "No. You eat too much junk food!"

Now the one thing Johnny liked more than liver and onions was candy! And the more he thought about it ... as he dragged his feet along slowly while trekking to the store was, "I want some candy! I need some candy! And I'm gonna buy some candy too!"

When he arrived at the supermarket he immediately went to the candy stand and bought so much candy that he had no money left over to buy the liver with.

In fact, he totally forgot the liver ... and as he was walking back home ... eating the candy to the last bite ... it occurred to him that he had not bought the liver.

My mother is gonna skin me alive! What am I gonna do? He pondered this dilemma as he passed a graveyard, where a funeral was just finishing up. And as folks were leaving the graveyard, a thought popped into Johnny's head: *I can sneak back here to the graveyard and dig up the corpse and take that liver!*

He continued to his home, where his mother had been waiting for the liver to begin her preparation of that night's meal. In walked Johnny ... without the liver.

"Johnny," his mother said, "where is the liver?"

"Oops," responded Johnny. "I guess I totally forgot!" He then ran back out the door ... snuck around behind the house to the tool shed ... where he retrieved a shovel and a large knife. He then proceeded back to the graveyard. It was getting to be dusk as he arrived. There was nobody around.

"This is gonna be easy," he said to himself as he began to dig in the soft earth. The grave belonged to old Mr. Walker, and when Johnny dug him up he was still fresh. Johnny turned up his nose—"Ugggh!"—and began to carve out old Mr. Walker's liver. He wrapped it in paper and trudged back home with the dripping prize.

Johnny's mother was again waiting at the door, where she immediately grabbed the package. "I've got to hurry because your father will be home soon and will be wanting his dinner."

When Johnny's father came home from work, the smell of liver and onions was in the air. He grinned a toothy grin, winked at Johnny, and said, "Sure smells good! Your favorite dinner, too, eh son?"

Johnny didn't respond. He began to feel sick as he tried to figure out how he was going to pass on the night's dinner.

When the table was set, Johnny's mom called out, "Dinner's ready!" as she rang the dinner bell. Everyone sat down ... Father said the prayer ... and dishes and cutlery began to rattle and ring around the table.

Johnny's father noticed that he was conspicuously passing up the liver and onions. "What's the matter, son?" he said. "You usually love liver and onions."

"I don't know, Dad," replied Johnny. "Must be something I ate previously ... I just don't feel like eating much just now."

Since Johnny usually ate up most of the liver and onions, his father was glad to have the lion's share of the dinner. In fact, he even remarked how especially good the liver was tonight. Johnny's mother said that it was OK if he wanted to leave the table, and if he wanted some later, it could be heated up.

Johnny half-heartedly agreed and went on upstairs to prepare himself for bed. He climbed the thirteen steps up to his bedroom ... quickly shed his clothes ... and thanked his lucky stars that he'd gotten away with the deception.

The night began to get darker, and the wind began to howl from an approaching storm. Johnny was at first frightened, as most kids are at an electrical storm, but the escapades of the day had worn him out ... and he soon fell into a troubled sleep.

At the stroke of midnight there was a CRASH! Johnny sat bolt upright in bed.

"What was that?" he said to himself.

The wind was really howling by this time, and several flashes of lightning split the night. "Must have been thunder," he convinced himself ... but he noticed that the front gate was swinging to and fro in the wind. Bam! Bam!

As he began to finally settle back down he heard ... almost as if on the voice of the wind,

"... J-o-h-n-n-y?"

"What?" he answered sleepily.

"J-O-H-N-N-Y?" The voice was a little louder now.

"W-w-what is it?"

"It's ME," answered a disembodied voice. "It's Mr. Walker, Johnny!"

"M-M-M-Mister Walker?" answered Johnny.

"Y-e-s," said Mr. Walker. "I want my liver back!"

"I-I-I-I d-don't have your l-l-liver, Mr. Walker!" exclaimed Johnny.

"Y-e-s, you do!" said Mr. Walker. "And I want it back!"

And with that Johnny heard the front door creak open. He heard shuffling noises as if feet were crossing the floor ... and then he heard in a spooky singsong voice,

J-o-h-n-n-y, I'm in your house!

Then Johnny heard footsteps on the stairs leading up to his bedroom.

J-o-h-n-n-y, I'm on your first step ...
J-o-h-n-n-y, I'm on your second step ...
J-o-h-n-n-y, I'm on your third step ...
J-o-h-n-n-y, I'm on your fourth step ...
J-o-h-n-n-y, I'm on your fifth step ...
J-o-h-n-n-y, I'm on your sixth step ...
J-o-h-n-n-y, I'm on your seventh step ...

Johnny began to whimper. "What am I gonna do?"

J-o-h-n-n-y, I'm on your eighth step ...
J-o-h-n-n-y, I'm on your ninth step ...
J-o-h-n-n-y, I'm on your tenth step ...
J-o-h-n-n-y, I'm on your eleventh step ...

Johnny pulled the covers up over his head...

J-o-h-n-n-y, I'm on your twelfth step ...
J-o-h-n-n-y, I'm on your thirteenth step ...
J-o-h-n-n-y, I'm in the hall ...
J-o-h-n-n-y, I'm at your door ...

Johnny began to sweat profusely.

J-o-h-n-n-y, I'm in your room ...

Johnny began to tremble uncontrollably as he whimpered out, "I don't have your liver...h-h-h-help!"

J-o-h-n-n-y, I'm by your bed ...
J-o-h-n-n-y ...
I've ...
GOTCHA!

Story Notes

I first heard this old traditional African-American tale when I was just a small child. My sister used to tell it to me as I lay trembling under the bedsheets. This is one of the so-called "shock" or "jump" tales, which are intended to be told in close proximity to the audience. In telling this tale it is important to use a droning, singsong chant when reciting ...

J-o-h-n-n-y, I'm on your first step ...
J-o-h-n-n-y, I'm on your second step ...
J-o-h-n-n-y, I'm on your third step ...

This will lull the listener into a semi-hypnotic state that will produce the desired result when you shout ...

J-o-h-n-n-y, I'm by your bed ...
J-o-h-n-n-y ...
I've ...
GOTCHA!

Enjoy!

JAMES "SPARKY" RUCKER has been performing stories and singing folksongs for close to forty-five years. With several albums to his credit, including the storytelling CD *Done Told the Truth Goodbye*, he has performed at every major folk and storytelling venue in the United States and Canada, including several appearances at the National Storytelling Festival. With his wife, Rhonda, Sparky has also performed in Europe, the United Kingdom, and in Australia. His published stories have appeared in numerous publications including *Appalachian Heritage* and *Sing Out!*, as well as August House's *More Ready-to-Tell Tales*. Sparky and Rhonda Rucker also contributed a chapter to the book, *Team Up! Tell in Tandem!* They live just outside Knoxville, Tennessee, and can be found on the web at www.sparkyandrhonda.com

Fearless Females

Aaron Kelly's Bones

Based on Appalachian and African-American Folklore
Kevin Cordi

Everyone knew Aaron Kelly.

Aaron Kelly was as mean as a three-headed snake—and his poison was even worse. He had a temper, and nothing ignited it more than seeing other men talk to his "Miss Alice." He called her his "prize"—not a prize like a tiara you parade around in a beauty contest but a prize like a hidden treasure you keep to yourself. Aaron Kelly tried his best to hide Miss Alice from everyone. He insisted Miss Alice was *his.*

"No one is going to take my prize away from me!" he would yell. "I will have the head of any man who tries."

Once, a man had commented to Miss Alice, "Madame, with that new hat you look as pretty as the sun." The whole town heard Aaron Kelly yell, "I will block out the sun if you ever say such words to my prize again!"

When Aaron Kelly arrived in town, people moved out of the way. Mothers grabbed their children. Grown men would quickly nod and just as fast run away when they saw him. It was said his eyes could dig deep into your very bones.

It seemed as though nothing affected Aaron Kelly—nothing, that is, except the passage of time. As the years passed, Aaron Kelly was disturbing the townspeople a little less and staying home a little more. Eventually he took sick and stayed in bed. Passersby could hear him coughing the next town over. Some said he did not have long to live, and in fact, he did not.

And during this time, no one saw Miss Alice. People believed she was trapped in their house.

☠☠☠

In fact, the next time anyone saw her, Miss Alice arrived in town wearing a coal black dress. She marched in Old Harris's funeral parlor and whispered, "Aaron Kelly is dead. Someone might want to know, but I doubt it." She then went in to the newspaper office and took out an obituary that read: AARON KELLY DIED TODAY AFTER A LONG SICKNESS.

It seemed that everyone in town came to the funeral except the fiddler. Mr. Henry played "Will the Circle Be Unbroken" at every funeral. On this day, the fiddle was silent. Aaron Kelly had more company when he was dead than he ever had alive. Some said they were there more out of curiosity than care— would the pastor be able to think of a single good thing to say about the man?

The only one to wear black was Miss Alice.

Old Man Phelps exclaimed, "I can't believe the old man is dead."

Others said, "I think he died five years ago, but his body didn't know it yet."

Young Tommy Bledsoe said, "I don't know if I could look at his grave. His bones would scare me."

Miss Alice did not cry. She paid her respects and left. A year passed, and Miss Alice never visited the grave of Aaron Kelly. She had no reason. It had been a year of quiet; no one had called her stupid or worthless. She only now knew it was safe to smile. No one called her a "stubborn mule" any more. Aaron Kelly's bones were in the ground.

☠☠☠

In the spring, Miss Alice planted a garden with new azalea bushes in the front yard. She liked to sit on the porch and anticipate the arrival of their blooms. She had tried to grow them once before, but Aaron Kelly pulled them out and called, "Old woman, they are weeds just like you." Then he would sneer, "They will die here, and so will you."

One day Miss Alice heard a knock on her door. When she opened it, there stood Mr. Henry, the fiddler, carrying a small sprig of flowers.

"Good evening, Miss Alice. My, you look lovely in your sun hat. I was wondering, perhaps, if it is not seen as impolite, would you care to join me at the country dance this Saturday? I would be most honored to have you as my guest."

Miss Alice looked at Mr. Henry and could not help but notice how kind he was to her. She agreed to go to the dance.

Meanwhile, the bones of Aaron Kelly started to itch.

At the dance, Miss Alice never stood still. Not only could Mr. Henry fiddle as good as a cat crawls, but when he was not striking at the bow, he could dance. Miss Alice felt safe in his arms. The dance did not end that night; it led to another night, another night, and still another night. They were soon dating—and dancing—on a regular basis.

The bones of Aaron Kelly continued to move.

Late one Friday night, the sun had gone to bed and only a sliver of the moon was awake. Miss Alice was home alone when she heard a strange, irregular sound at her door. It sounded less like a knock than a scraping.

When Miss Alice opened her door, her smile left for good. Standing in front of her was not a living thing at all but a skeleton. On the skeleton's arm she saw Aaron Kelly's old broken wristwatch. It was the same one that she told him to fix but he said, "It ain't broke if I can still wear it." She knew then this skeleton was dead old Aaron Kelly, making a house call.

The skeleton glared at her and said, "Woman, I told you I would return if you ever saw another man. This is my house, and you are my woman, and here is where I am going to stay."

The skeleton walked to the rocking chair and began to rock, back and forth, back and forth.

"Look here, Aaron Kelly, you have to leave. You died. It's not right for you to be here."

"Nonsense. Dead or alive, I am staying right here," said Aaron Kelly.

"You have to go now."

"I am not budging."

Meanwhile, Miss Alice spied Mr. Henry from her big bay window, walking down the lane. She had asked him to teach her how to strum a few notes, and he was late arriving. Miss Alice pleaded with the bones to leave.

"Woman, fix me something to eat. Your food is worse than the worms, but I am hungry," Aaron Kelly snarled.

Miss Alice fed Aaron Kelly some simmering hot soup, but it spilled out through the bones, washing away to the living room floor.

"Aaron Kelly, I have fed you. Now it is time for you to go."

About this time, Mr. Henry knocked on the door. Miss Alice tried to ignore it, but Aaron Kelly yelled, "Open the door, woman! Don't you have any manners?"

Reluctantly, she opened the door. Miss Alice's face was pale.

"Miss Alice, what is wrong?" Mr. Henry inquired.

Miss Alice simply pointed to the rocking chair.

When he saw what was in the chair, Mr. Henry was speechless. Slowly he took Miss Alice's hand. Both of them watched as the skeleton rose from the rocking chair.

"Henry, you and your case need to leave now. Mark my words, you cannot have my woman as long as I remain in this house. You need to stick to fiddling. I intend to stay, so you best be gone!" declared Aaron Kelly.

"She never was your woman," Mr. Henry responded. "You treated her like property. You say you love her, but you don't, because you don't know what love is. I love her, and I intend to stay as long as she will have me."

Miss Alice stammered out some words. "Aaron, Henry is right. You never bought me flowers, you never noticed my smile, and you never cared for me. I was more like a slave than a wife. Leave, Aaron Kelly. I do not love you and I never have."

"What good would it have been to bring flowers to you?" bemoaned Aaron Kelly. "All they are are weeds in fancy dress!"

The hours whittled by. Miss Alice and Mr. Henry did not know what to do. Each minute ticked away as they watched the bones rock back and forth, back and forth.

Finally Mr. Henry stood up. "Aaron Kelly, you said I should stick to fiddling, and that is just what I am going to do." He turned to Miss Alice and whispered, "Since we missed the dance tonight, I will bring the dance to you."

With that, Mr. Henry opened his case, took out his fiddle, and began to play. "Miss Alice, sometimes you have to go on and leave the hard times by," he declared. "Let us have some fun." He then struck up "Turkey in the Straw."

No one could play like Mr. Henry. Just hearing his music made your toes tap. Even the bones of Aaron Kelly began to jiggle. Next he tuned up "The Mountain Whippoorwill."

He played stronger and stronger.

Not only did Aaron's toe bones begin to tap, his whole skeleton began to twist, turn, and sway to the music. Aaron Kelly began to dance, and Mr. Henry played faster. Soon a thigh bone flew from the skeleton and hit the fireplace. As the music got louder and stronger, his elbow bone hit the ceiling.

"Play harder, Mr. Henry, play harder!" yelled Miss Alice.

Bones flew everywhere. The leg bone hit the cat box, and the kitty slunk screaming into the kitchen. A finger bone sailed into the living room. A toe bone hit Grandpa's portrait. Some bones flew by the cabinet, some under the rocker, some outside. Bones were everywhere.

Mr. Henry played on and on.

Miss Alice began to scoop up the bones one by one and stash them into an old flour sack. She and Mr. Henry hurried to the graveyard, where they spent the rest of the night burying the bones in four different plots. She saved one bone in the sack. The night air was quiet.

Six months later, Miss Alice and Mr. Henry married. On their wedding night, they placed the small bone Miss Alice had saved above their fireplace. They hardly ever raised their voices with each other, but on the few occasions when they did, they stopped when one or the other of them would notice the bone above the fireplace.

Meanwhile, in that graveyard, it is said, the bones still move. But it's a fool's tale, because once something is dead he or she is dead.

Ain't that right?

Story Notes

This tale has roots in Appalachian and African-American folklore. I found a much lighter version in a picture book, The Dancing Skeleton *by Cynthia C. DeFelice and illustrated by Robert Andrew Parker (New York: Macmillan, 1989); another version is found in a collection of folktales by Harlem Renaissance poet Langston Hughes. Like any good folktale, each time it is written or told it changes.*

When telling the story, have fun with it. Allow yourself to play with the shaping of the story. Experiment with using contrasting intonations to communicate the voice and manner of Aaron Kelly, Miss Alice, and Mr. Henry. Use carefully placed pauses in your narrative, taking an extra second or two to create suspense at critical places. This is especially true when Aaron Kelly's skeleton is knocking on the door. In previous versions of this tale, Miss Alice's voice is not heard. In this version I worked to give her a voice. Think of another eerie tale and how you might make it stronger by enhancing a minor character. As you finish telling this tale, may your bones stay quiet.

KEVIN CORDI is a nationally and internationally known professional storyteller and teacher who loves a good frightening tale. He is a Ph.D. candidate at The Ohio State University, studying the importance of story and drama in learning. He has heard this Appalachian tale for years as he toured around the country. It never fails to make him and students wonder and laugh at the same time. You could say people go to pieces when they hear it. You can find out more about Kevin's work at www.kevincordi.com and www.youthstorytelling.com.

The Snow Ghost

Based on Irish and Scottish Folklore
Wendy Welch

When Mary was born, her mother lived just long enough to kiss her baby girl goodbye. Her heartbroken father took the newborn to his sister, Jean, and her husband, James.

"How can I raise a baby?" he asked. "There's nothing I know about babies. Help me."

And of course, they did. Baby Mary was snuggled into the family alongside her cousins and grew up like a daughter in the house. Her father went north to find work in farm country, but he came back every weekend to see his baby girl and brought Jean and James money for her keep.

☠☠☠

One day Mary's father was driving a threshing machine, and one of the moving parts stopped moving. When he went back to see what was wrong, there was an accident—and now Mary was an orphan.

Just three years old, Mary was too young to understand much of this, but her aunt told her the story, cuddling the girl on her knee. Mary wanted to hear the story again and again as she grew up. Aunt Jean always ended it the same way: "So now you're a daughter in this house and will be all your life. And that's the end of that."

It was the end, Mary thought, but she always felt odd that she couldn't remember much about what her father looked like.

She'd been so young when he died, and there was no photograph, not even a wedding picture.

☠☠☠

So Mary grew up looking after her younger cousins and helping Jean in the kitchen, playing with her schoolmates and living on the small farm, called a croft, that kept the growing family supplied with food. Mary was now the middle child in a large family, all boys except for her. Sometimes, as they cooked and cleaned and mended, Aunt Jean would reach out and rub the back of her hand on Mary's cheek. "It's good to have a daughter in the midst of all these sons," she'd say. Without ever putting it into words, Mary knew that was Jean's way of saying she wasn't just here to work, and that she loved her.

☠☠☠

One day, when Mary was about fourteen, Aunt Jean called her into the parlor. It was a frightening thing to be summoned to this cold, clean room with its good furniture, too special to use every day. The parlor was reserved for the minister and other important guests, or for a talking-to from Aunt Jean before Uncle James took you out back to cut a switch off the birch tree. In her mind, Mary ran through what she could have done wrong as she walked into the parlor.

Aunt Jean took one look at her expression and burst out laughing. "Dearie me, don't look so scared! I only want to talk to you, Mary. Sit here." She patted the sofa beside her.

When Mary sat down, Jean took her hand and held it a moment before speaking. She didn't look at Mary.

"Daughter of mine," said her aunt, "it's not the end of the world, but it's hard times, that's sure. Your uncle can't get work, and I can't go myself since the twins were born. They're too young to be without me all the day. But you, Mary, you're a great strong lass."

Her aunt looked at her, and Mary was surprised to see pleading—and tears—in her eyes. "We need you to go to work and bring your wages home. We'll get through this bad patch, but we need money. There's a family in one of the great houses wanting a maid. It's a bit far, the other side of Edinburgh, but you can stay there during the week and come home Saturdays. It's all arranged, if you say yes. But if you don't want to go ..." Aunt Jean did not finish the sentence; she just looked at Mary.

Mary tried to keep a grin from her face. She could see that her aunt was upset, but Mary was excited. The city! A big house! A chance to see how other people lived, to leave the croft ... Maybe there would be a girl her own age in the house. Mary could feel her face breaking into a smile and bit her lip hard to stop herself.

Aunt Jean was a smart woman. She gave a rueful laugh and squeezed Mary's hand. "Well, if that's the way of it, we'll have James take you across on Monday." She leaned over and kissed the top of Mary's head. She had to stretch up to do it. Mary was a tall girl.

On Monday morning James took his niece to the house, a long ride in a borrowed pony cart. Mary carried Aunt Jean's gold-handled carpetbag. Inside it were two spare dresses, her nightgown, and the rag doll Aunt Jean had made for her when she was a wee girl. She'd meant to leave the rag doll home, now that she was a grown woman working in town, but at the last minute she'd wanted it so badly—she couldn't say why—that she hid it under her nightgown in the bag.

She bid her uncle a cheery goodbye and ran up the steps to the house. She didn't look back, but Mary could hear Uncle James turning the cart and the slow crunch of the wheels across the drive, and she knew he was looking back at her. She gulped down the fear in her throat, straightened her back, and knocked on the big oak doors.

An angry voice came from the lawn. "Here, you! Don't use the main doors; they're for your betters. Go 'round to the servants' entrance. What's wrong with you, country bumpkin, are you stupid?"

A man was standing at the side of the house. No, not a man, but a boy about Mary's age, big for his age. Hands on his hips, face red with anger, he stared at Mary as she approached. His clothes were expensive—clean and perfect. Mary knew at once he was a son in her employer's family. She started to stammer an apology. The boy snarled, "Get away!" and swung his walking stick at her. She ducked and ran to the servants' entrance at the back.

Mary soon learned that the young man—Donald McGrath—was best avoided. The cooks, the groomsmen, the butlers, and the other maid all rolled their eyes and shook their heads when his name came up. Once, sitting in the kitchen talking to the cooks, the head butler called him an "impertinent little boy." Mary didn't know what *impertinent* meant, but she liked anyone calling such a self-important person a little boy—especially when he was so big.

So the weeks went by. Mary slept in a little room under the attic eaves and spent her days cleaning, sewing, sometimes even cooking. She loved the kitchen, with its warm smells and welcoming smiles from the cooks, and would linger there as often and as long as possible. But she worked quickly in the parlor, the drawing room, and any other place where she might be caught alone by Donald McGrath—who would as soon slap a servant as say good morning to her.

And every weekend, Mary went home. One day, when they were baking bread together and Mary had her sleeves pushed up to work the dough, her aunt noticed a bruise on Mary's arm. "How did you come by that, dearie?"

Embarrassed, Mary pulled her sleeve down. "Och, clumsy me," she said. She knew her aunt and uncle were feeding the family with the money she brought home, now that winter had set in. She wasn't going to complain or tell her aunt how Donald liked to wait at hall corners to jump out and scare her so badly she would upset the mop pail. How he would run away laughing, leaving her to clean up the mess. Or how he snuck behind her as she started the morning fire in the great downstairs fireplace and yelled so that she jumped up and hit her head on the stones.

No, there was no point in saying anything about awful young McGrath. Mary was clever enough to avoid him most of the time— and tough enough to accept what came her way when she couldn't.

☠☠☠

One night Mary stumbled to her bed later than usual. One of the cooks was sick, and she'd been lending a hand in the kitchen. Bone-weary, she didn't see a shadow move in the hallway. Out stepped Master McGrath and gave her a shove. She fell into the railing of the staircase, smacking her ribs so the breath flew out of her.

"Sneaking 'round in the night! Trying to steal something, no doubt!" he snarled.

Mary's patience snapped. "Let poor honest working folk get to bed, you great overgrown bully. For shame—master-to-be in this house and not the manners of a schoolboy! Uncle James would whip you 'til you couldn't stand!"

Donald's eyes widened. His face grew dark. "You can't talk to me like that!" he shrieked and launched himself at her.

She was against the stair railing, and as he came at her, Mary knew two things: she couldn't fall, and she couldn't let him fall, no matter how badly she wanted to. Whoever fell would be killed.

She was a great strong girl; her aunt had said so. Planting her feet, Mary held onto the rail as he slammed into her, grabbed him by his nightshirt as he teetered, and held him upright. Swaying but not falling, she pushed him, hard. He landed safely on the hall floor, sliding on his backside across the polished surface to the far wall. In fury he leapt up and tackled her again, this time grabbing her arm as if to wrench it from the railing.

Mary felt a sharp burning encircle her elbow. She gasped. She'd never felt pain like that. They both heard the sharp crack at the same moment. He let go, but it was too late.

Mary grabbed at her arm, wincing as she touched it, reeling sideways to avoid the stairs. Donald stood wide-eyed a moment, then turned and ran, yelling, "Thief! Thief!"

Her arm throbbing, her head muddled with pain, Mary didn't think; she just moved. Down the staircase she ran, cradling her arm against her side with her other hand. The great oak doors were closed and barred, but there was no stopping her. The beam that barred the door, which required two men to put in place, she flipped up with one mighty thrust and barrelled through the doorway. She fled into the snowy night as the cries of the waking household faded behind her. She was running, running like a frightened animal, away from that house, away from that boy, toward home.

But home was a long way away, and it was dark and cold and snowing. Mary was wearing only her maid's uniform, and now her arm throbbed so badly she could hardly draw breath. She looked around. Nothing was familiar. With a sinking feeling in the pit of her stomach, Mary realized she was lost.

"What do I do now?" She spoke into the empty air, but from the darkness a voice answered.

"And what is it you want to do, young Mary?"

She was too tired even to turn and see who was speaking to her. In a whisper that was half whimper she said, "I want to go home."

"Then home it is," said the man appearing at her side. He was stocky, not much taller than she was, his black hair shot through with gray. He held out a hand to her, then drew back. "I do not like the look of that arm. Let me see."

Shaking from cold and fear, Mary stood silent, but when the man touched her arm, she winced. "Hmmm," he said. "This will hurt, but then it will feel better." He touched her arm again, and it burned, then stopped. Her arm still throbbed, but it was a dull ache, not the sharp pain of before.

"Now, let's get you home to Aunt Jean, young lady." He held out his hand, and she took it. There was nothing left to say or do. She was cold, she was tired, and she wanted to go home.

They walked, and he talked, asking Mary about the school at her aunt's village and what Mary had learned there, asking after the young cousins and the croft. But he never asked her about the big house, or why she was standing in the snow with a broken arm. And Mary was so tired she really didn't notice when, in the early light of dawn, she swayed on her feet and started to fall. She didn't react when the man picked her up like a rag doll and carried her the rest of the way to Aunt Jean's, laying her down in the doorway.

Such a fuss was made! The whole household got up, the little cousins dancing around, bringing blankets and warm clothes. Jean dressed Mary in a dry flannel nightgown and got some hot tea down her while the young ones pulled woollen socks over her feet. Sitting on the floor in front of the fire, Jean tucked Mary into the quilts and rocked her in her arms until she fell asleep, safe and warm.

☠☠☠

It was late morning when Mary awoke in her aunt and uncle's bed. The first thing she saw was her aunt, sitting in a chair by the bed, smiling at her. She smiled back.

Aunt Jean spoke. "Well, now. Mr. McGrath's been 'round with your bag and two months' wages." Her mouth set in a hard line. "Seems to think there's been a misunderstanding, and he doesn't want the police involved." She shook her head, then smiled at Mary again. "So you'll not go back to that place. Just you lie there, and I'll fetch you some tea." Aunt Jean brought two mugs, then settled into the chair. "Now, start at the beginning, and tell me everything."

So Mary started with the boy on the lawn, talked through the cooks in the kitchen and Master McGrath breaking her arm, and finished with the man who'd saved her from freezing to death. Jean looked angry, then confused, and finally concerned.

"Mary, love, you've had a rough time. Your arm's got a bruise the size of a horse's hoof, but the bone's not broken. And no one brought you home. There were your own footprints in the snow and we found you crumpled like a rag doll in the doorway. It broke my heart, seeing you so. You walked here alone. It was a snow dream you were having."

Mary shook her head. "No, he was real. He was just as tall as me, and his hair was black and white together. And when he touched my arm, it stopped burning."

Aunt Jean looked at Mary, a strange expression on her face. "Tell me, did this man have anything here?" She pointed to the side of her cheek.

Closing her eyes, Mary concentrated, remembering. "A scar, almost to his chin, like a half-circle."

At that, Aunt Jean sat back. "Och, that's the way of it," she said as if to herself. "No doubt your arm was broken, and he fixed it." She turned her attention back to Mary and gave a swift smile. "The man who brought you home, dearie, he was your father."

Story Notes

At my friend Liz Weir's festival in Northern Ireland, I met a storyteller named Mrs. Quigley, who told an Irish version of this story. The idea of a ghostly helper appearing to get a family member out of trouble is fairly well known in ghostlore. The returning ghost is called a revenant, and it serves one of two purposes: revenge, or making amends. In the revenge stories, the revenant can be quite violent, but in the making-amends variants, as in this one, the ghost helps the family member out of a difficult situation.

When telling this story, it helps to put on some characteristics of each person. Jean is a nice, warm woman—and desperate. Mary is an excitable yet sensible young girl. Master McGrath is a spoiled brat who doesn't understand the consequences of his actions. How would each speak a little differently than the other? How would each move—or hold still—while speaking? It helps to think a little bit about what each character wants and how he or she feels about what is happening as the story unfolds.

DR. WENDY WELCH teaches Cultural Studies at the University of Virginia's College at Wise and runs a used bookshop. She and her husband (who is from Scotland, where this story is set) travel the world singing and telling stories. They have two dogs, two cats, and 24,000 books. Wendy has served on the boards of both the U.S. and U.K. national networks of storytellers. She likes to swim, crochet, eat lunch with friends, and write.

Pretty Maid Ibronka

A Hungarian Folktale
Mary Grace Ketner

Hungary is the land of the vampire, but this folktale tells of another strange and evil creature—an oopir. *And what is that? Find out along with Ibronka.*

Many years ago, in a village, there lived a girl named Ibronka, who was very pretty. In fact, everyone called her "Pretty Maid Ibronka"—but pretty as she was, she had no sweetheart. When the girls gathered to spin and to sew in the evenings, most of them had sweethearts who came and sat and talked with them as they spun. But no one came to sit with Ibronka, until at last one day she said, "If only God would give me a sweetheart, even if a devil he were!"

That night, all the girls came to Ibronka's house to spin, and soon their sweethearts came to join them. When all were settled in as usual, to their surprise there came another knock at the door. In walked a young man wearing a sheepskin cape and a cap with crane feathers. He came and sat at Ibronka's side and began talking only to her. So nervous and pleased she was that she dropped her spindle. She leaned over to pick it up and, feeling about for it, her hand chanced upon the young man's foot, and she could tell that it was not a foot at all but a cloven hoof. Later that night, when they were saying goodnight, they embraced in the way of the young and Ibronka noticed that her hand did not hold to his back but crossed right through his body.

The next morning Ibronka went to see a wise old woman of the village and told her about all the strange things that had happened the night before. "And now, kind mother," Ibronka asked, "put me wise? What should I do?"

The wise woman told her to go not with the same circle but to other spinning groups. And that Ibronka did, but wherever she went the young man appeared. She tried politely to discourage him, but, night after night, he sought her out.

So Ibronka returned to the wise old woman. "Old woman," she said, "I shall never get rid of him this way. Who is he? And whence does he come, for I am afraid to ask him."

"Well, then," said the old woman, "learn a trick from the young girls who cannot yet spin but wind the thread on spools. Tonight, when you are saying goodnight to him, pretend some awkwardness, and as you fumble with your fingers, run a needle threaded to a spool of thread into the back of his sheepskin cape; then as he leaves, unwind the spool until it stops. Then follow the thread and wind it up, and in this way, you will find where he lives."

That night, the spinning was to be at Ibronka's house. When the girls and their sweethearts had arrived and another knock came at the door, they all stopped in silence and expectation. In walked the young man and sat at Ibronka's side. And when the evening was over, and they all had left, the sweethearts walking the girls home, Ibronka and the young man drew close to each other. As they embraced and talked about this and that, Ibronka sewed her needle into the back of his sheepskin cape.

At last they said goodnight, and as the young man went his way Ibronka began to unwind the spool. Fast did the thread unwind, and Ibronka began to speculate how much more there could be, and just then, the thread stopped and no more came off the spool.

Then Ibronka began to rewind it, walking as she wound, wondering where the thread could be leading her. It led her straight toward the church.

Well, she thought, *he must have passed this way.*

But the thread led her further on, straight into the church and to the door that opened to the churchyard, the cemetery. The moonlight shone in through the keyhole. Ibronka bent down and peeped through the keyhole, and whom did she behold there, standing beside an open grave, but her own sweetheart! And what was he doing? As she watched, he lifted the head of a man from the grave and sawed it in two, separating the two halves, just the same way one might cut a melon in two, and then she saw him feasting on the brains from the halves. Seeing that, she broke the thread and in great haste made her way back to her house.

But her sweetheart must have caught sight of her and briskly set out after her. No sooner had she reached home and bolted the door safely on the inside than she heard her sweetheart calling to her through the window:

> *"Pretty Maid Ibronka, what did you see*
> *When you put your pretty eye to the hole for the key?"*

When she heard those words, she was terrified! So terrified that—well, she lied.

> *"Pretty Maid Ibronka, what did you see*
> *When you put your pretty eye to the hole for the key?"*

> *"Nothing did I see!"*

> *"Tell me, or your sister will die!"*

> *"If she dies, then we'll bury her,*
> *But nothing did I spy."*

Then nothing. No sound.

Ibronka did not sleep that night. Next morning, her sister did not wake.

Ibronka went to the old woman. "Old grandmother, I need your advice." And again she recounted the strange events of the night before. "What shall I do?" she asked.

"Now listen," said the old woman. "Take my advice and put your sister in the cellar."

Ibronka did that, and that evening, she did not dare to go out to spin, but stayed at home, and what should happen? Her sweetheart came again to the window!

"Pretty Maid Ibronka, what did you see
When you put your pretty eye to the hole for the key?"

"Nothing did I see!"

"Tell me, or your mother will die!"

"If she dies, then we'll bury her,
But nothing did I spy."

That night, Ibronka did not sleep. In the morning, her mother did not wake. Ibronka put her mother in the cellar.

And that night, as she waited fearfully at home, her sweetheart came again:

"Pretty Maid Ibronka, what did you see
When you put your pretty eye to the hole for the key?"

"Nothing did I see!"

"Tell me, or your father will die!"

"If he dies, then we'll bury him,
But nothing did I spy."

That night, Ibronka did not sleep. In the morning, her father did not wake.

She took her father to the cellar, and then went as fast as she could to the wise old woman. "Old grandmother," she said. "Give me some comfort in my distress. What is to become of me?"

"There is nothing you can do. Can't you see where this is leading? You are going to die. Now, go and tell your friends to come to your house tonight. And when you die—because die you will for certain—they must not take the coffin out either through the door or the window."

"How then?"

"They must cut a hole in the wall and push the coffin through that hole. And they should not carry it along the road but cut across through the gardens and the bypaths. And they should not bury it in the cemetery but in the ditch beside the churchyard."

Well, Ibronka went home and sent word to her friends, and they appeared when she called and sat with her.

In the evening, her sweetheart came to the window:

"Pretty Maid Ibronka, what did you see
When you put your pretty eye to the hole for the key?"

"Nothing did I see!"

"Tell me at once, or you shall die!"

"If I die, they will bury me,
But nothing did I spy."

For a while, she and her friends kept up the conversation. The friends were only half inclined to believe that she would die, and at last they all nodded off and went to sleep. But when they awoke, they found Ibronka dead. They were not long in bringing in a coffin and cutting a hole in the wall and passing the coffin through it and carrying it off—not on the roads, but cutting across the gardens—and they buried her in the ditch beside the churchyard.

The next night, Ibronka's sweetheart went to the house. He asked, "Doors and Windows, was it through you that they carried Ibronka?" and the doors and windows answered, "No, it was not."

He went to the road and said, "Was it over you that they carried her coffin?" and the road answered, "No, it was not."

He went to the churchyard and asked, "Tell me, Churchyard, was it in your ground that they buried Pretty Maid Ibronka?" and the churchyard answered, "No, it was not."

As he did not get any wiser from the doors and windows, the road, or the churchyard, he said to himself, "Well, I see I shall have to find out for myself. I shall get myself some iron sandals and a staff, and I shall search for her until I wear them out."

☠☠☠

Now, it happened that over her grave in the ditch beside the churchyard, there grew a beautiful white rose, and one day a boyar was riding by in his coach and saw it and went to pick it. When he arrived home, he placed it in a vase of water. He put the vase in front of a mirror on a sideboard of his dining room, so that he might look upon the rose even as he ate.

That night, he became full before he finished his supper. "Leave the food on the table," he instructed his servant. "I may come back and eat it later."

Next morning, his servant said, "I see you came into the dining room last night and finished the food."

And the boyar said, "No, I did not. I thought you ate it."

The next night, the leftover food disappeared just as it had the first night the boyar brought the rose home, and when the same thing happened again on the third night, he decided to wait up and watch, thinking he would catch his servant in a lie. He hid himself in the dining room, and when all was still, he saw the rose arise from the vase. It began to quiver, then to shake, then transformed itself into a beautiful maiden—the loveliest he had ever seen. He watched as she ate, so gracefully, he thought, so delicately, and he began to fall in love with her. Then she stood from the table and began to quiver, then to shake, and he feared that she would change her form again. Hastily, he came out of hiding and took hold of her, grasping her tightly in his arms. "You must marry me," he said, "for I have fallen in love with you."

The girl insisted that she could not, but he pressed her further, saying that she must do so.

Finally she agreed but set one condition: "You must never ask me to go to church with you."

The boyar said, "There will be none of that, though I may go by myself sometime."

And so they were married and lived quietly, the boyar and the girl, who, you must have guessed, was Ibronka. After a few years, she had a child, a son, and after a few more years, she had another. Her husband took the boys to church with him, but Ibronka never went with them.

Now this might have been fine, but, well, you know how it is with people! They said to the boyar, "Why is it that you bring your sons to church with you, but your wife never comes?" He would make some excuse or other for her, and, as there was always some new reason, tongues began to wag. The question began to wear on him until one day he said to Ibronka, "Won't you come to church with me and our sons?"

"You agreed that you would never ask me to do that," she said.

"Must we abide by that old bargain forever?" he asked. "Come with me."

"Very well," she said. "But no good can come of this." And she went to dress for church.

When Ibronka joined her husband and sons, it made the people rejoice to see them. "That is the right thing to do," they said among themselves.

At the end of the mass, as they were leaving, a man came up the aisle wearing a pair of iron sandals, worn to holes, and carrying a rusty iron staff in his hand. He rapped it on the floor until it broke. Then the stranger spoke. "I pledged to myself, Ibronka, that I would put on a pair of iron sandals and take up an iron staff and go out looking for you, even if I should wear them to naught. At last I have found you. Tonight, I shall come for you."

On the way home, the boyar said to his wife, "What did he mean?"

"Never mind," she replied. "You shall see."

But Ibronka was no longer that young maid who felt unloved. She had a husband who called her "my dear" and two sons who called her "mother," and she did not wish to hear the question that she knew the *oopir*—for that is what he was, she now knew—would put to her again.

That night, he came to her window and asked:

"Pretty Maid Ibronka, what did you see
When you put your pretty eye to the hole for the key?"

And Ibronka said: "I was the prettiest girl in the village, but I had no sweetheart. Once, I let it out that I wished God would give me one, even if one of the devils he were! There must have been something in the way I said it, for that evening when we gathered to do our spinning, myself and my friends and their sweethearts, there appeared a young lad in a sheepskin cape with a hat graced with the feather of a crane. He greeted us and took a seat at my side, and when I dropped my spindle, my hand chanced to touch his foot, except it was not a foot at all but a cloven hoof! Then when I embraced him, my hand passed right through his body ... *but it is a dead and not a living soul to whom I am speaking.*"

And all the while, he stood outside her window, shouting at the top of his voice, drowning her words:

*"PRETTY MAID IBRONKA, WHAT DID YOU SEE
WHEN YOU PUT YOUR PRETTY EYE TO THE
HOLE FOR THE KEY?"*

"I sought advice from a wise woman in the village, and she
told me to go to a different house to spin, but he followed still.
Then she told me to pass a needle with thread through his cape
and unwind the thread as he left and to follow it and rewind it
to find out where he lived. I did that and followed him to the
church and into the churchyard, the cemetery."
And he was outside overshouting her:

*"PRETTY MAID IBRONKA, WHAT DID YOU SEE
WHEN—"*

"But he must have seen me, for he followed me home and
demanded I tell him what I saw—"

*"WHEN YOU PUT YOUR PRETTY EYE TO THE
HOLE FOR THE KEY?"*

"And through my fear, I brought about the deaths of my
sister and my mother and my father, *but it is a dead and not a living
soul to whom I am speaking!*"

"PRETTY MAID IBRONKA, WHAT DID YOU SEE—"

"But now I tell you that I looked through the keyhole, and
in the moonlight—"

*"WHEN YOU PUT YOUR PRETTY EYE TO THE
HOLE FOR THE KEY?"*
"I saw him cut in half the head of a corpse, just as I might
cut a melon in half—"

"PRETTY MAID IBRONKA, WHAT DID YOU SEE—"

"And place each half to his lips—"

"—PUT YOUR PRETTY EYE TO THE HOLE FOR THE KEY?"

"And he—*YOU!*—drank the brains, *but it is a dead and not a living soul to whom I am speaking!*"

And when he heard this, the *oopir* uttered a cry which rent the night and shook the castle to its bottom, and he collapsed beneath the window.

And when Ibronka looked to where he had been standing, there was nothing but a patch of scorched earth. She turned away from the window, and there saw standing behind her her husband and sons, and behind them her sister, her father, her mother.

The spell was broken at last, and she knew ... she knew ... that she would not hear it again:

"Pretty Maid Ibronka, what did you see
When you put your pretty eye to the hole for the key?"

Never again!

Story Notes

"Pretty Maid Ibronka" is well known in Hungary. The strongest version I've found was told by an agricultural laborer named Mihály Fedics and recorded by folklorist Gyula Ortutay in 1938; it can be found in English in Folktales of Hungary, *edited by Linda Dégh (Chicago: University of Chicago Press, 1965).*

This story is a cautionary tale, a juicy bit of gossip about something that someone else did wrong ... and you don't want to make the same mistake! Tell it just the way you would relate a scandal that happened to a girl in your school, someone people might even envy just a bit. After all, Ibronka is the prettiest girl in the village! Who wouldn't want to know about the time she asked for trouble, then lied about it, then got herself into a worse fix? You are the one who knows all the sensational details; dole them out temptingly, and in your own words, just the way you would tell friends about someone who got sent to the principal's office for smoking in the restroom. Keep that tone until you get to the rhyming couplets; they should be memorized exactly and chanted in a jumprope rhythm, changing voices as the oopir confronts Ibronka repeatedly, and she repeats her lie. That singsong conversation—the oopir's demand and Ibronka's frightened lie—will interweave to chill your listener to the bone.

Storyteller MARY GRACE KETNER develops and performs programs of world folktales, fairy tales, and legends for school, religious, and civic audiences. Her published works include magazine articles and stories, teaching units and curriculum kits for elementary and secondary schools, and a children's book, *Ganzy Remembers*. For a decade, Mary Grace was director, scriptwriter, and one of several storytellers for the daily radio show *LIFETIMES: The Texas Experience*, aired by more than fifty stations throughout Texas. With two degrees in education and experience as a teacher, religious educator, and museum educator, Mary Grace advocates storytelling as a transmitter of human values in all her work. She lives in San Antonio, Texas.

Mia's Ghost

An Original Story
Robert D. San Souci

Best friends Brent and Kristi were sitting on Brent's front porch steps. It was a late afternoon very near Halloween. Dried leaves scuttled down the sidewalk. The nine-year-olds were resting after riding their bikes, which were laying side-by-side on the lawn.

Kristi looked up at the pumpkin perched on the porch rail. "You made that really scary," she said.

"Thanks," Brent said. "My dad helped. Mom wanted a funny face, but my dad likes scary things—just like me."

"I *love* being scared," Kristi told him.

"Oh, yeah!" Brent agreed. Then he sighed. "My mom doesn't like me watching scary movies or stuff. But when she works late at her office, my dad and I watch them. Only I have to promise not to tell. The other night we saw one about a haunted house that had thirteen different kinds of ghosts in it."

"Were they scary?"

Brent shrugged. "Some were kind of stupid. But there were a couple of really creepy ones."

"I'd like to see a real ghost," Kristi said.

"That would be cool," Brent said. "But there are no such things as real ghosts."

"I can show you one," someone said.

The two friends jumped a little. They hadn't seen the stranger—a girl about their own age—wander up the path from the sidewalk.

"Who are you?" asked Brent, feeling a little silly for having been startled.

"Mia Burns," the girl answered. "I live a couple of blocks away." She waved her hand toward Maple Street. "I just wanted to get a better look at your pumpkin—it's really scary—but I heard what you were saying about ghosts. I can show you a real one."

"Can you?" Kristi asked eagerly.

But Brent said, "She's making it up. There are no ghosts."

"Cross my heart," said Mia. And she did.

"Show us," said Kristi as she stood up. When Brent kept sitting, she grabbed his hand and pulled him to his feet. "You too!"

"Come on *now!*" Mia insisted. "This is the right time of day to see the ghost. It only stays for a short time. I think that's because the person whose ghost it is may have died about this time."

The girl hurried down the sidewalk, waving impatiently for Brent and Kristi to follow. The other two, catching something of her excitement, ran after her.

Mia led them up one street and down another. When she stopped, Brent and Kristi found themselves in a strange neighborhood.

"So where's this ghost?" asked Brent. He and Kristi were panting from all the running.

"Right there!" said Mia, pointing at a rundown house across the street.

"It *does* look kind of creepy," Kristi observed. Weeds had overgrown the front yard. Paint was peeling off the wood everywhere. The lower windows were boarded up; some of the upstairs windows, which had not been covered, were broken out—probably by kids throwing rocks. Black graffiti was scribbled everywhere. Clearly, no one had lived in the house for a long, long time.

"Are you going to come?" teased Mia. "Or are you afraid?" She looked carefully both ways and then darted across the street.

Brent and Kristi crossed the street more slowly. "I think she's going to trick us," Brent whispered. "She's going to pretend she sees a ghost or yell just to scare us."

"Maybe," said Kristi. But she didn't sound so sure. Brent could see that Kristi truly wanted to meet a real ghost. He, on the other hand, wasn't sure *he* was quite so keen on an encounter. Side by side, the friends followed the other girl up the crumbling, weedy brick path to the front door.

"Can't we get in trouble for being here?" asked Brent. Now he clearly sounded not at all sure that he wanted to take things further—let alone come face-to-face with a *real* ghost.

"We're just looking around," said Mia, clearly annoyed that he was being so hesitant. "And how could we mess things up any more than they are already?"

"Yeah." Kristi shot an impatient look at Brent. "Don't be such a wuss."

Mia nodded to show she was glad the other girl had taken her side. Then she smiled, "Besides, I know the family who lived here. They've been gone a long, long time. It's clear they don't care about this place anymore."

"But it's locked," said Brent. "We can't get in."

"Check this out," said Mia. To the surprise of the others, she turned the knob and the front door opened with a loud *creak*. Grinning, she turned around and said, "Don't be afraid. The ghost won't hurt you."

Hand in hand, Brent and Kristi followed her into the shadowy, dusty hall. Whatever furniture had once been there was mostly gone; the rooms they saw only had a few broken chairs and tables in them. It was hard to see anything because the windows were boarded over. Some early evening sunlight filtered in through cracks between the boards; gray light from above partially lit the big staircase to the second floor.

Mia didn't even look back to see if they were behind her when she climbed the squeaky old stairs. Silently, Brent and Kristi followed—on the alert for anything startling or creepy that might be hiding in the shadows to leap out at them or suddenly make a grab for their ankles through the stair railings. Brent kept waiting for Mia to grab him or yell "Ghost!" or do something stupid to scare them. But no grasping ghostly hands or frightening figures appeared; their guide continued up the steps without even a single look back, her eyes focused on the landing above.

The upstairs proved as disappointing as the lower floor—just broken chairs and narrow tables against the walls. The dirt and dust on the unbroken window panes were so thick that everything seemed dim. Dead moths were piled on the windowsills; a few flies buzzed and bumped desperately against the glass. Otherwise, nothing moved or made a sound.

"Where's the ghost?" Brent asked, feeling braver now that nothing had appeared. They were standing in the upstairs hall that stretched dark and cobwebby to the right and left.

"Let's look in the rooms here," Kristi suggested. But though they peered into every doorway that opened off the hall, they saw nothing but a few more bits of furniture, tons of dust and mouse droppings, and dirty, bare windows glowing red from the sinking sun.

Now Brent was feeling sure enough to say to Mia, "Your ghost is a big fat zero."

Mia smiled. "I guess it's not going to show up today. You can never tell with ghosts."

"You just made up the whole story," said Kristi. To Brent she said, "We'd better get out of here before we get in trouble."

All the way down to the front door, Brent waited for Mia, who was following them, to try one last trick. But she didn't. When they were back on the front porch, the girl closed the door carefully behind them.

"I guess you still don't believe in ghosts," Mia said, with the biggest smile yet.

"No way!" said Brent while Kristi just shook her head.

"Well, you're both wrong," Mia said, as she faded into the cool autumn air.

Story Notes

This story is an original, but it has its roots in the many old folktales—some no longer than an anecdote—in which someone who disbelieves in ghosts meets a person who discusses the issue quite matter-of-factly, then—in a quick twist of an ending—reveals that he or she is the final proof of the existence of ghosts, since he or she is a ghost him- or herself. The revelation most usually takes the form of the second party's vanishment in front of the hapless onlooker.

For the story to be most effective, a certain amount of authorial (or storyteller's) use of "misdirection" is necessary. In the case of "Mia's Ghost," the emphasis is on the details of the "haunted" house, and the lingering suspicion that Mia is going to try to fool Brent and Kristi. Hopefully the last sentence, whether read or told, will come as a surprise twist—which also reveals the second meaning in the story's title. Mia is both teasing her friends about the idea of a ghost, while she is in fact Mia's ghost. This story might make a nice "campfire" tale with a great little "stinger" at the end.

ROBERT D. SAN SOUCI is the author of award-winning books for younger readers—many of which adapt traditional folktales, fairy tales, and ghost stories for new audiences. He is the author of such well-known picture books as *The Talking Eggs*, *Cinderella Skeleton*, and, most recently, *As Luck Would Have It*, illustrated by his brother, Daniel San Souci. A lifelong fan of shuddery tales, he has published two popular series of scary stories: the "Short & Shivery" books, which retell traditional national and international weird tales, and the "Dare to Be Scared" series of original stories. He also wrote the screen story for the Disney animated feature *Mulan*. He lives in the San Francisco Bay area.